D.J. bent to look closely into the roots of a ponderosa that had fallen in a snowstorm last season. He swallowed hard and reached out his right forefinger to scrape the dirt away from what he'd seen. Breathing hard, he yanked off his glove and used his bare finger and thumb to pick up the small object.

Unbelieving, D.J. rubbed it against his sturdy winter jacket. The object in his fingers looked like a small, heart-shaped yellow rock. It was about the size of a half-dollar overall, but it was much, much heavier. The color was what excited the boy most.

Eagerly, he glanced down again. He bent quickly and picked up another object, slightly smaller than the first. This one was longer with a slight curve like a crab's claw.

"GOLD! Gold nuggets! Two, maybe more! Alfred, I've found an old abandoned *gold* mine!"

LEE RODDY is a best-selling author of more than 50 books. He lives in the Sierra Nevada Mountains of California and devotes his time to writing books and public speaking. He is a co-writer of the book which became the TV series, "The Life and Times of Grizzly Adams."

Born on an Illinois farm and reared on a California ranch, Lee Roddy grew up around hunters and trail hounds. As a boy, he began writing animal stories. He spent lots of time reading about dogs, horses, and other animals. These stories shaped his thinking and values before he went to Hollywood to write professionally. His Christian commitment later turned his writing talents to books like this one.

This is the seventh book in the D.J. Dillon Adventure Series.

The Mystery of the Black Hole Mine

LEE RODDY

VICTOR BOOKS

A DIVISION OF SCRIPTURE PRESS PUBLICATIONS INC.
USA CANADA ENGLAND

THE D.J. DILLON ADVENTURE SERIES

THE HAIR-PULLING BEAR DOG
THE BEAR CUB DISASTER
DOOGER, THE GRASSHOPPER HOUND
THE GHOST DOG OF STONEY RIDGE
MAD DOG OF LOBO MOUNTAIN
THE LEGEND OF THE WHITE RACCOON
THE MYSTERY OF THE BLACK HOLE MINE
GHOST OF THE MOANING MANSION
THE SECRET OF MAD RIVER
ESCAPE DOWN THE RAGING RAPIDS

5 6 7 8 9 10 11 12 13 14 Printing/Year 00 99 98 97 96

All Scripture quotations are from the *King James Version* and from *The Living Bible*, © 1971 by Tyndale House Publishers, Wheaton, IL 60189. Used by permission.

Library of Congress Catalog Card Number: 87-81003
ISBN: 1-56476-508-3

CONTENTS

1. Finding the Gold Nuggets   7
2. A Terrible Surprise   15
3. When a Boy Remembers   22
4. Nails Abst Comes Back to Town   34
5. The Secret of "Crazy" Calhoun   43
6. Chased by Shadows   54
7. Sharp Words Between Friends   63
8. A Second Sharp Disagreement   69
9. Dad Clamps Down   77
10. Danger Deep in the Mine   84
11. Terror in the Tunnel   94
12. Out of the Blackness   104
13. A Christmas to Remember   115
   Life in Stoney Ridge   122

To
my daughter-in-law,
Katie O'Shaughnessy-Roddy
and
my son-in-law,
Alfredo de Haas
for enriching our family

Chapter One

FINDING THE GOLD NUGGETS

D.J. Dillon was easing along a narrow deer trail on
the steep slope of Jawbone Ridge when it happened.
He lifted his eyes from the dangerous ledge for a
moment to glance back. He wanted to make sure that
he and his friend Alfred had lost whoever was
following them. Subconsciously, D.J. could hear his
little dog Hero baying on a trail off in the distance.

As the thirteen-year-old boy took another step
without looking, the decomposed granite suddenly
collapsed under his feet.

"Oh, no-o-o-o!"

The eighth-grader threw up his hands in a vain
effort to stop his fall. Brush ripped through his leather
gloves and tore his heavy waist-length jacket. He felt
his face being scratched, but the mountain boy
couldn't slow his plunge.

It was only about a ten-foot fall which was broken
by the dense underbrush. Still, D.J. smashed through

everything to land flat on his back in a small ravine. His blue stocking cap had slipped over his face.

Tiny flecks of light exploded in his head and floated before his eyes. Dust swirled into his nostrils and choked him. He heard small rocks and gravel sliding down. He realized he could be buried alive— but for a moment, he was powerless to move.

He lay there stunned, staring up at the gray November sky and wondering if he were paralyzed. Only his mind seemed to work.

He heard Alfred calling as if from a great distance. "D.J., where'd you go?"

Actually, D.J.'s best friend had only been a few feet behind him around a curve in the great mountain's side when D.J. fell.

"Here, Alfred." The words came out as a muffled whisper through the cap over D.J.'s face.

Alfred Milford sounded concerned. *"Where?* I can't see you!"

D.J. tried to sit up, but he couldn't move his arms or legs. Frightened, he opened his mouth and called weakly.

"Here, Alfred!" This time his voice was stronger. "Down here!"

"Down *where?*" Alfred sounded closer.

"Below the ledge." D.J. got his hands to move. He shoved the cap off his face so he could see.

A moment later Alfred's head appeared in the opening in the brush overhead where D.J. had fallen through. Alfred's red stocking cap and upturned coat collar blocked out the weak autumn sunlight.

"D.J., what in the world are you doing down there? We're wasting time because whoever's chasing us could be closing in. . . . "

D.J. interrupted. "The trail gave way and I fell. Look out that you don't fall down too!"

For the first time, his twelve-year-old friend seemed to realize D.J.'s problem. Alfred used his right thumb to push his owlish glasses farther up on his nose. His glasses looked as thick as the bottom of a soda pop bottle.

"You OK, D.J.?"

"I . . . I think so." The tiny shooting stars before his eyes were gone. D.J. sat up slowly and pulled the warm cap over his head and down below his ears. His blue eyes focused on the ledge above.

"D.J., can you climb out by yourself?" Alfred asked anxiously.

"Just a minute." He reached out and took hold of a black oak sapling. He pulled himself to his feet. Rapidly, he checked himself over.

D.J. was taller than anyone in his classroom at Stoney Ridge Grammar School in California's high Sierra Nevada Mountains. He was half a head taller than Alfred, who was a year younger and a grade behind him.

"I'm fine," D.J. called, glancing up. "Jarred my whole body, and I'm scratched up some, but I'm OK."

"Take my hand and I'll pull you up."

"No, that's all right. I'll just step on this old timber. . . . "

There was a creaking and snapping as D.J. put his leather boot on the almost-black wood. It was barely visible in the tangle of underbrush.

"Careful!" Alfred called down. "Doesn't sound very strong to me."

"I'll find another way up. Hey, Alfred—you know what this looks like?"

"Can't see it from here."

"Like a headframe* from an old gold mine!"

The derrick-like structure had fallen from its former upright position to the ground where wild blackberry vines and other brush had totally hidden it.

"I've heard there are some up in these mountains left over from the Gold Rush days. But I didn't think the Mother Lode* was this high in the mountains," Alfred said loudly. "I thought it was down a thousand feet or so in the foothills."

" 'Gold is where you find it!' " D.J. quoted a common saying in the Mother Lode. "Maybe there's still some gold left here!"

Alfred warned, "Watch out for the mine shaft!* It's probably close by, hidden under all that brush! Some of those shafts go straight down several hundred feet. If you fall down *there,* you'll miss Christmas!"

D.J. grinned at his friend's humorous warning of a very serious fall. He glanced around the brush.

"I don't see the mine opening, but it *must* be here somewhere. Hey! Wait a minute!"

D.J. bent to look closely into the roots of a ponderosa* that had fallen in a snowstorm last season.

Alfred protested, "Don't stop to look now! That guy who's following us could come back into sight any moment!"

D.J. barely heard. He didn't answer. He swallowed

---

*You can find an explanation of the starred words under "Life in Stoney Ridge" on pages 122–129.

hard and reached out his right forefinger to scrape the dirt away from what he'd seen. Breathing hard, he yanked off his glove and used his bare finger and thumb to pick up the small object.

Unbelieving, D.J. rubbed it against his sturdy winter jacket. The object in his fingers looked like a small, heart-shaped yellow rock. It was about the size of a half-dollar overall, but it was much, much heavier. The color was what excited the boy most.

D.J. quickly wet his left forefinger in his mouth and rubbed the object. The brightness improved. He popped one end of the object into the corner of his mouth and bit gently. He felt it give between his teeth. That was confirmation it was soft. A rock would not give even a tiny bit.

"It *is!*" he breathed. *"It is!"* Eagerly, he glanced down again. He bent quickly and picked up another object, slightly smaller than the first. This one was longer with a slight curve like a crab's claw.

"What're you talking about, D.J.?"

D.J. looked up, his face shining. He excitedly brushed away pale, yellowish hair that spilled down from under his cap. He held up his find.

"GOLD! Gold nuggets! Two, maybe more! Alfred, I've found an old abandoned *gold* mine!"

Alfred could resist no longer. He found a foothold and carefully climbed down to where D.J. was standing.

The excited boys eagerly searched for more nuggets, their unknown pursuer forgotten. When they didn't find any more gold, they searched for the mine. Six-story-tall conifers* grew in the ravine and head-high brush had grown thick as a jungle.

The boys were within six feet of the massive mountain's sheer face when D.J. pointed.

"There! That's it!"

"Where?" Alfred peered hard through his thick glasses. "Oh! I see it! Boy! A person could pass right by and never notice that mine opening!"

The friends quickly but carefully moved dense brush aside and finally stood before the mine opening. It was an ugly black hole totally hidden in the ravine. It reminded D.J. of a bad tooth cavity he'd once had.

Breathlessly, the boys cautiously peered into the threatening blackness. They couldn't see more than a few feet into the entrance. They wisely stayed out of the mine.

D.J. cried, "See how tall those trees are in front of the mine entrance? I'll bet nobody's been here for 70, maybe 100 years! It's probably been abandoned so long I can legally file on it."

Alfred grinned so widely his face seemed likely to split. "I'm sure this is public land, so we'll be rich! Rich! RICH!"

D.J. had started carefully replacing the brush so the mine's opening would again be totally hidden from even a few feet away. Alfred's words gave D.J. a funny feeling.

He wanted to say, *It's mine! I found it!*—but he was surprised and ashamed of his thought.

Aloud, he said, "We've got to keep it a secret! You know what happened when word got out that James Marshall had discovered a few flakes near here!"

"Yeah! The California Gold Rush of 1849! We also can't tell anybody until we can file a claim."

D.J. frowned. Alfred had said it again: *"We."*

Alfred promised, "We won't tell anybody! Sure's we do, the word'll get out and somebody will try to jump* our claim!"

"Come on!" D.J. cried, ignoring the funny feeling about Alfred laying claim to part of the mine. D.J. shoved both the nuggets deep into his right front pants pocket. "Let's get out of here so we can talk about what to do next!"

The friends took quick but careful landmark bearings so they could find the place again. D.J. started to whistle for his dog Hero, but stopped abruptly.

"Hey! If I do that, whoever's been following us will hear and know where we are! We'd better get away from here first."

"I'd forgotten about that!" Alfred glanced around anxiously. "Wonder who it is and why he's following us?"

D.J. frowned. "Do you suppose he knows there's an old abandoned gold mine around here and he's been looking for it?"

Alfred pursed his lips thoughtfully. "Well, these mountains are full of strange people, hermits and such. Hey! What was that?"

"What was *what*?"

"There!" Alfred pointed back the way they'd come. "I saw a light reflect off of something."

"I don't see anything."

"It's gone now. Maybe it was the sun reflecting off a rifle barrel, or maybe the sun hitting the glass on a pair of binoculars! D.J., he may have seen us find the mine!"

"Let's get out of here!" D.J. cried.

The boys clambered back up to the trail and hurried down the long, jawbone-shaped mountain. They ran for a long time. They were nearing the edge of dense trees near an open meadow when they finally stopped. Out of breath but feeling safe, they collapsed to rest against the great trunks of ponderosas. D.J. was ready to whistle for Hero.

Suddenly, there was vicious sound: "Hiss-thunk!"

It sounded like an arrow whizzing through the air and striking the tree above D.J.'s head. He glanced up. A short bolt-like object quivered in the trunk just above D.J.'s head.

Involuntarily, both boys drew back.

A voice called harshly from behind a tall sugar pine.*

"That's your *only* warning!"

D.J. swallowed hard and managed to speak up. He couldn't see anybody. "We're not doing any harm! We're just giving my dog a run. . . . "

The voice interrupted. "You heard me! Now get out of here—and don't *ever* come back!"

The boys didn't answer. They sprinted out of the threatening trees and across the open meadow.

D.J. heard Alfred panting behind him and moaning, "D.J., we've got big troubles!"

Chapter Two

A TERRIBLE SURPRISE

D.J. didn't like leaving his little hair-pulling bear dog* in the mountains, but Hero knew his way home. Hunters often went home, leaving their hounds running a trail, and the dogs always found their way back.

So D.J. and Alfred hurried through the rapidly fading afternoon light, knowing Hero would be home by morning.

The short dusk came early after Thanksgiving at the 3,500-foot elevation of California's Sierra Nevada Mountains. D.J. and Alfred had to reach their homes before full dark. That was the deadline both sets of parents had set for the adventuresome boys.

Yet it was hard for D.J. and Alfred to stand at the edge of the little lumbering community of Stoney Ridge and part for the evening.

"What'd you think, D.J.?" Alfred asked for perhaps the tenth time. "Did whoever it was that ran us off the mountain see us find the gold?"

As he had before, the older boy shrugged. He was tall and thin, but he seemed shorter and bulkier with his shoulders hunched against the rising cold wind.

"I don't know, Alfred—but I doubt it, though, because we'd run a long way from where we last saw him until I found the nuggets."

"He could have been watching us through binoculars," Alfred replied. "And he caught up with us to fire that . . . that . . . whatever it was at us."

D.J. shook his head. "Whoever he is and whatever he wants, we've got to get into Indian Springs and find out how to file a claim before *he* does.

"But tomorrow's a school day, so there's no way I can talk my dad into taking me to the court house at Indian Springs."

Alfred said, "It'll probably be Saturday before we can get to town, and then the court house will be closed! D.J., we've got to get there *before* Friday!"

"Well, right now I've got to get home or I'll be grounded."

"You know what, D.J.? Sooner or later, we've got to go back up on that mountain—past where that *thing* was fired at us. That's the *only* way to the gold mine."

"Shh!" D.J. whispered, looking around at the small town's deserted streets. "Don't say *gold!* You know what happened when people heard that word back in 1849!"

Both boys had studied California history in school. They knew that when James Marshall had found some gold flakes at Sutter's Mill in a nearby county, thousands of people from all over the world had flocked to the foothills. The 1849 Gold Rush had almost immediately turned remote, sparsely populated California into a state with a booming population.

"Gold fever's like that," D.J. added. "So remember—not a word to anybody!"

"Not a word!" Alfred promised solemnly. He turned toward his home on the opposite end of town. Then he swung back. "I'll look up that funny arrow in my reference books when I get home. But I'm pretty sure it's a bolt fired from a crossbow.* I've heard about them somewhere."

"Wish we'd pulled that thing out of the tree and taken it with us," D.J. said, frowning thoughtfully. "But I'm sure it's every bit as dangerous as a real arrow."

Alfred suggested, "Make a list of all the things we need to do when we get to the county seat."

D.J. nodded, waved, and hurried toward home, walking on the left side of the main street's high concrete sidewalk. He mentally clicked off the things that had to be done to protect his mine. He had a scary feeling he was already in a race with someone he didn't know and hadn't seen.

As he neared the town's only general store, D.J. stopped short. A big kid was clomping down the sidewalk from the opposite direction. His heavy boots echoed off the front of the store. D.J. stared, trying to see better. The town's old-fashioned street lights had come on, but they were too weak to show anything clearly except the Christmas decorations.

"That looks like Nails Abst!"* D.J. told himself, catching his breath. The memory of how mean Stoney Ridge's bully was made D.J. stop and wait to be sure.

"It is!" he muttered. "I thought he and his father had moved away!"

D.J. started to cross the deserted street to avoid Nails. Nails entered the store without seeing D.J., who continued across to walk on the opposite sidewalk. D.J. glanced across the street as he passed the store. He could see Nails inside the lighted front window.

Wonder why Nails is back in town? D.J. thought. Wow! Sure glad I didn't meet up with him today or tonight!

He broke into a jog to beat the darkness home and make sure he didn't see Nails again. As D.J. crossed the last main street intersection just before starting up the steep hill toward home, he heard a car round the corner behind him. The car's headlights illuminated the Christmas decorations which squeaked softly from lampposts and a wire strung across the street.

Ordinarily, D.J. wouldn't have even thought about a car coming up behind him. However, the afternoon's events had made him nervous. He broke into a full run.

Behind him, D.J. could hear the tires kicking up late autumn leaves from the street. The boy felt the short hairs on the back of his neck begin to stand up with fear.

The car didn't slow as it drew up behind D.J. He started to sigh with relief when the brakes squealed slightly. The headlights cut sharply to the curb behind him.

Fear rose inside his body as D.J. remembered the warning voice in the forest.

"Oh, no! He's stopping. Come on, feet! Faster!"

D.J. felt adrenalin* stream through his body like
hot melted lead as the car's headlights turned the
boy's shadow into a monstrous black thing. Then the
shadow dropped off to the side as the car pulled up
even with the boy.

D.J. considered cutting across a vacant field when
a man's voice boomed from the car's dark interior.

"Is that you, D.J.?"

The boy slowed and stopped. He turned to face
the street. His heart began to slow and his breath
became more even. He stepped to the curb and
looked into the open front window.

A giant of a man leaned over from the driver's
side. D.J. recognized the deep, booming voice. It
belonged to Paul Stagg, the lay pastor of Stoney
Ridge's community church.

Even though the boy couldn't see clearly inside the
darkened sedan, he could discern the outline of the six-
foot, four-inch tall man. He was probably wearing
his usual blue jeans and saddle-colored cowboy boots.

"Jump in, D.J., and I'll give you a lift home."

Eagerly and with great relief, the boy opened the
right front car door. The dome light came on and he
saw Kathy Stagg in the backseat. The lay preacher's
thirteen-year-old daughter smiled.

"Hi, D.J.," she said, tossing her red-gold hair in
characteristic fashion. It fell down both sides of her
freckled face and onto her blue and white winter
jacket.

"Hi, Kathy," D.J. replied.

He picked up Brother Paul's white ten-gallon
Stetson* hat from the seat and slid into the car. D.J.
rested the hat on his lap and buckled the seat belt.

He closed the door with a great sense of relief.

"You were sure running hard, D.J.," Kathy continued with a light tone to her voice. "Something after you?"

Her father eased the sedan away from the curb. His voice rumbled up from his big chest like distant thunder. "Now, Kathy, don't you go teasing D.J.! You know he was just trying to get home so his folks wouldn't worry!"

D.J. slumped into the safe comfort of the car. He decided to change the subject.

"Been Christmas shopping?" he asked.

"Just getting back from Indian Springs." The big man's pleasant voice filled the car. "Kathy had some dental work done and was feeling a little bit under the weather, so she's been stretched out in the backseat."

"Where have *you* been, D.J.?" Kathy asked, leaning forward behind him.

"Oh, I was just out exploring with Hero and Alfred."

He tried to make it sound casual, but he wanted to shout, "And we found gold! And an old gold mine!" But he kept the secret.

She asked, "Where's Hero?"

"Still out there following some trail. But he's done that before and come home safely by himself."

Kathy seemed satisfied. "What're you giving your family for Christmas?"

"I don't know yet." He felt the weight of the two gold nuggets in his pocket and thought that they could probably make this the best Christmas ever.

In a few minutes, Brother Paul eased the sedan to

the high concrete curb in front of the Dillon home. "Give my regards to your family, D.J."

D.J. knew it was suppertime, and it was bad manners not to invite friends in, even unannounced. "Aren't you coming in?"

"My missus will have supper waiting," Brother Paul replied. "Much obliged, anyway."

D.J. waved as the Staggs' car pulled away from the curb. He ran around the side of the house to see if his little dog had beaten him home. But the doghouse was empty and quiet.

D.J. opened the back door to the kitchen and tried to look casual—as though he hadn't just discovered a gold mine.

The thought was blown out of his mind at the sight of his father, stepmother, and stepsister sitting dejectedly at the small kitchen table. D.J. saw instantly that Two Mom's nose was red and her eyes were bright from tears.

D.J. had never felt comfortable calling his stepmother "Mom" or "Mother." So he called her "Two Mom" because she was his second mom.

"What's the matter?" D.J. asked.

Dad was a short, powerfully built man who rarely showed emotion. His cheek muscles twitched as he tried to speak, but couldn't.

D.J. was scared. "Dad? Two Mom? What's *wrong*?"

Neither answered, but nine-year-old Pris let out an anguished squeal and ran to him.

"Dad lost his job and we're going to have to move away from Stoney Ridge!"

Chapter Three

WHEN A BOY REMEMBERS

Pris threw her arms around D.J.'s waist in a most unusual way. For a moment, he stared down at the top of her head.

"What?" he asked, glancing at his father and stepmother.

Dad still didn't say anything. He rose and went into the living room. D.J. pried Pris' arms loose from his waist and followed Dad.

Still in silence, the man bent and picked up a pair of long-cuffed asbestos gloves. He slid them over his powerful, work-hardened hands and kneeled in front of the glass-fronted stove. As he opened it, the blast of extra air made flames leap higher within the firebox.

"Dad?" D.J. bent to look his father in the eyes. They seemed strangely shiny and moist. Dad did not look up. He picked up an eighteen-inch long round of dry live oak and laid it inside the stove.

22

The boy turned back to the kitchen. "Two Mom, what's going on?"

In the months Dad and Two Mom had been married, D.J. had never seen his stepmother cry. But now her eyes were bloodshot and tears were sliding down her cheeks.

Two Mom's hands flew about nervously like two birds trying to escape. "Oh, D.J.! Your father just got home. . . . "

He waited for her to continue, but she rested her elbows on the table and suddenly buried her face in her open palms.

Almost sick with anxiety, the boy spun back to his stepsister. She was still standing numbly by the back door.

"Pris, *you* tell me," he demanded.

As always, her brown hair looked untidy, like an eagle's nest that had fallen onto a fence post. Her voice was shrill as she looked up at D.J.

"It's just what I said, D.J.! Dad lost his job, and we're going to have to moo . . . moo . . . move! And I don't want to move away from my friends!"

"Move? Move where?" D.J. cried.

"Maybe to Sacramento!" Pris wailed.

D.J. was shocked. Mountain-born and reared, he found the idea of living in a city in the flat valley below the Sierra Nevadas terrible.

"Dad, I can't move away from Alfred—especially just before Christmas!"

Dad's voice struck with the force of a slap. "David Jonathan Dillon, do you think I *want* to move? You think I wanted to lose my job?"

Dad's voice seemed to explode as he reentered the

kitchen with quick strides. He jerked the asbestos
gloves off.

"I've worked for that lumber company practically
since before you were born! But they're closing the mill
and laying everyone off! Foreign competition, they
said! So we've got to go where I can get work, and you
know there's nothing in Stoney Ridge and probably
not much possibility at Indian Springs! So that means
Sacramento!"

Two Mom laid a hand on her husband's strong
forearm. "Easy, Sam," she said softly.

D.J. gulped and absently took off his coat to hang
on the peg by the back door. Indian Springs wouldn't
be too bad. The county seat was just a dozen miles
or so down the mountain in the foothills. D.J. would
have to ride the bus there to high school each day
when he finished at Stoney Ridge Grammar School. But
Sacramento?

He asked, "When?"

"Soon's I can find work," Dad replied dully. "They
laid us off at quitting time tonight, without warning."

Pris wailed, "But it's almost Christmas!"

The four Dillons glanced at each other, then at the
calendar hanging near the refrigerator. D.J. said
quietly, "Less than a month."

Two Mom tried to smile. "It'll be OK," she said as
cheerfully as possible. "The Lord will take care of us;
He always has." She brushed the back of her right
forefinger gently across her eyes and continued.

"He took care of Pris and me when my husband
was killed in that logging accident. God took care of
you, D.J., when your mother died in that auto crash.
Now we're a family, and He will take care of us in this

situation too.

"So," she continued firmly. "I'll finish fixing supper while the rest of you get washed up."

D.J. looked at his father. Sam Dillon nodded soberly. "Sure doesn't look too promising, Hannah, but we've been through worse things. We've got to trust."

Pris brightened too. "Could we have a family hug and a prayer?"

D.J. saw his father hesitate. Pris was asking for something brought from her first home when her father had been alive and she was Priscilla Higgins. Dad would never have done that before Two Mom and he married. Still, D.J. was pleased when Dad nodded and held his powerful arms out wide. His wife quickly stepped inside the comfort of his right arm. Pris moved to Dad's left.

D.J. hestitated, stung by the sharp way his father had spoken. Slowly, D.J. walked to stand beside his stepsister.

D.J. felt his father's calloused hand tremble as it gripped the boy's shoulder. D.J. started to close his eyes but stopped abruptly.

"What about Grandpa?"

Dad glanced at his son. "He's naturally welcome to move wherever we go. But he's got a mind of his own. So we'll find out what he wants to do first thing in the morning when we pick him up for church."

* * * * *

There was a gray "snow" sky the next morning when D.J. went outside to the backyard to check on his dog. Hero gave a joyful bark and rushed out of his doghouse next to the detached garage.

"I knew you'd come home OK!" D.J. said, kneeling to clutch the little mutt in his arms. "Yeah! You're a good dog and always come home!"

Hero wasn't much for looks, as Grandpa Dillon would have said. The dog was a mixture of hound, airedale, and German shepherd. He had a long black nose that stuck out from his muzzle a good half-inch beyond what it should have. He had the tan color of an airedale and a short, stub tail. To D.J., Hero was the best dog in the world.

The boy tried not to think about what would happen to Hero if they moved into the city. Two Mom was allergic to dogs, so Hero couldn't stay inside which would be necessary if they got an apartment in Sacramento.

"We've got to find a way to stay here!" D.J. told the little dog fiercely, ruffling his ears. "And we will!"

The boy had changed pants but transferred the nuggets to the pocket of the fresh pair. He felt the gold nuggets' weight against his leg. He couldn't say anything, but the gold offered the best way to stay in Stoney Ridge—if the mysterious follower in Jawbone Ridge hadn't also discovered the mine.

"Sure wish I could tell Grandpa," D.J. told Hero. He gave the dog a final pat and went inside to dress for Sunday School.

The four Dillons left early and drove into the country to pick up Grandpa Dillon and tell him about what had happened.

Driving along the winding mountain road, D.J. felt a little better than he had last night. If he had really found a gold mine, it didn't matter if Dad had lost his job.

All night long, D.J. had wanted to ease his family's concerns by telling them about the gold. But a secret was a secret, so D.J. kept his promise to Alfred and didn't say a word about the gold or the mysterious voice that had threatened the boys.

Dad drove his family onto a rough but paved country road. He parked on the dirt shoulder near where Dad, Grandpa, Mom, and D.J. had lived before Mom was killed and Dad later married Pris' mother.

It gave D.J. a strange feeling to see familiar places that now he might have to move away from and never see again.

He jumped out and quickly ran to the little unnamed creek. Two slender Lombardy poplars stood silently beside the bubbling stream. They were nearly bare for winter except for one yellow leaf near the top of the tree nearest the creek.

"Dad, the water's low enough that we can cross on the railroad ties the men at church put in when they rebuilt Grandpa's house. This bridge is easier to cross than the stone ones we had when we lived here and. . . . "

D.J.'s voice trailed off. He had almost said, ". . . when Mom was still alive." But the boy didn't want to say that.

Once a person was dead, it seemed people didn't mention them very often; especially when there was a new marriage and a "blended" family, as someone at church had called them.

The house had been rebuilt after a forest fire. But the surrounding ponderosas, oaks, cedars, and other trees that had stood in majestic splendor on the hill were now ugly and black. Even those trees not burned had died from the terrible heat. Acres of dead trees now stood where all had once been green and beautiful.

There was no driveway up to the house which was about a quarter mile up the steep hill and hidden just beyond the hilltop. The boy ran easily across the footbridge of blackened timbers.

Dad held Two Mom's and Pris' hands and helped them ease gingerly across the same bridge. D.J. reached the other side and started running up the rutted pathway toward Grandpa's house.

Dad called, "I'll tell him about everything, D.J."

"OK!" he called and began running up the rutted excuse for a path that led to Grandpa's home. He felt a whole lot better about things now that he remembered the gold, but he still had to make sure he could file on the claim. He was desperate to get to Indian Springs in case whoever had followed Alfred and him now also knew the mine's location.

When D.J. topped the rise, leaving the rest of his family far behind, he heard Grandpa's dog, Stranger, bark. He ran out from under the low front porch, trailing a long chain from his collar. Stranger "raised a ruckus," as Grandpa would have said.

The dog had been a stray that the old man befriended. Stranger was medium height, mostly white with some black splotches. He was probably part pointer, but he was no prizewinner.

His button ears, roach back,* ewe neck, and crank tail made Stranger about as ugly a dog as D.J. had ever seen. But Stranger made it possible for Grandpa to have a companion so he could live alone as he wanted, way out in the country. D.J. was glad for that.

As the boy drew near the house, he saw Grandpa talking to an unknown man. The two men were standing in a burned-over area behind the house near the first stand of dead trees. They glanced up at the dog's bark. D.J. slowed uncertainly, but Grandpa recognized him and waved him over.

"This here's my grandson D.J.—and this is Ora Octavius. He's hired on to help old man Crabtree who owns all the land around here that burned, 'cepting this house and a third-acre around it. Mr. Crabtree told Ora here to bring me a message, which he just done."

"Howdy," D.J. said. It seemed more grown-up to say what Grandpa always said.

Mr. Octavius blinked and drew back slightly as D.J. approached close enough to shake hands if the man offered to do that. Sometimes people shook hands with boys the age of D.J., and sometimes they didn't.

This man didn't. He had the look of an outdoorsman, but he wasn't a catalog-looking one. He had the gaunt, thin look of a person who didn't eat well. He hadn't shaved for days and his heavy coat and pants smelled as though they hadn't been washed in a long time. His brown eyes, hidden under the sagging brim of a sweat-stained old felt hat, somehow looked strange to D.J.

Mr. Octavius didn't even speak to D.J., but turned to look back at Grandpa Dillon.

"Let me know what you decide, Mr. Dillon," the man said. "I'll pass the word on to the boss."

He started walking rapidly away, across the rolling hills toward the nearest standing dead trees.

Grandpa called, "Wait and meet the rest of my
family! They're coming up the hill."

"Can't." The man's word came back, but he didn't
turn around. He walked away with ground-eating
strides.

"Unfriendly jasper," Grandpa said. "Wouldn't
even shake and howdy with you. He's the kind of
man you stand upwind from. Funny thing, I've heard
tell of Ora for years, but never laid eyes on him until
today."

"How come I've never seen him before, Grandpa?"

Grandpa led the way back toward the house. "I
hear he lives somewhere up in these mountains. Don't
rightly know where. Some folks say he's a little loose
in the attic from batching* all these years while he
roams through the hills. A little strange, all right.

"Comes down out of the hills sometimes to make a
little money doing odd jobs, like now, when he's
working for Crabtree. When Ora's got enough eating
money to last him a while, he disappears back into the
mountains."

"Something about him seems familiar," D.J.
replied.

"Just forget about him being downright
unfriendly, D.J. He didn't mean no harm; he just ain't
had no raising, I reckon. Well, come on in the
house. Soon's your father and the womenfolk get here,
I'll tell you what Ora wanted."

D.J. watched the man disappear beyond a little
rise before Dad, Two Mom, and Pris topped the hill
from the creek.

The boy followed his grandfather as he limped
toward the house. The old man walked with the aid of

what he called his Irish shillelagh.* It eased the
weight off of his arthritic hip. He wore a bright
green and red "Christmas color" tie, a double-breasted
blue serge suit coat long out of style, and a pair of
baggy brown slacks. Grandpa didn't think about
how clothes looked.

D.J. smiled at his small, feisty grandfather. There
was a special bond between the two that never existed
between father and son, though the boy desperately
wanted to have the closeness with his dad that he had
with Grandpa Dillon.

"Howdy, Stranger," D.J. said as he came up to the
dog chained to the front porch. He was answered with
a sloppy slurp of a wet tongue. "Hey!" D.J. cried,
jerking back his hand, "I already had a bath today!"

Grandpa chuckled and peered over the top of
wire-rimmed bifocals. He set his Irish shillelagh
against the back of his favorite old cane-bottom
rocking chair. It still rested on the porch by the front
door. Grandpa held out two age-spotted and
wrinkled hands.

"I been needing a hug for a powerful long time,
D.J. Got one left?"

The boy nodded soberly. "Guess I could spare
one."

D.J. grabbed his grandfather around the chest and
felt the old man's thin arms encircle him. They
trembled a little. D.J. thought a hug was about the
nicest feeling in the whole world.

Grandpa dropped his arms as the rest of the Dillons topped the rise and headed toward the porch.

"Sam!" Grandpa called. "Hannah and Pris! Right
glad to see you all! I've got some news!"

Pris skipped ahead of the others. "We got news too!"

"Priscilla!" Two Mom called warningly.

Grandpa didn't seem to notice. He picked up his cane and waved it in a broad sweep at the family stopped on the small porch.

"See all them there dead trees? Fellow name of Crabtree who owns all the land they're on sent word today by Ora Octavius. D.J. met him.

"Well, Crabtree said he wants the land cleared for reseeding new trees. He said if we'uns would cut them dead trees down, we can keep seventy-five percent of all we can make selling the firewood. Crabtree keeps the quarter share."

Dad didn't answer. D.J. saw him push into the front door. "Let's go inside where we can talk," he said.

A few minutes later, Dad had told his father about the mill closing, being laid off, and probably having to move to the valley near Sacramento to find work.

Grandpa didn't say anything for a moment. D.J. glanced around, feeling soft and warm inside. This was almost exactly like the house where he had lived with his mother, father, and grandfather before the car accident. The original house had burned down in a forest fire. After the fire a duplicate had been dismantled across town and rebuilt here by the men of Stoney Ridge.

To the boy, this was the closest thing to a permanent home he'd ever had. He didn't want to move away.

His thoughts were interrupted by Grandpa tapping the toes of his shiny black "Sunday-go-to-meeting" shoes with the rubber tip of his cane.

"Well, I'm obliged for you a'thinking of me kindly that way, but I'm going to stay here till the good Lord calls me home! Now, let's get to church!"

D.J. led the way out of the house and down the hill. He was glad Grandpa wasn't going to move, but the boy didn't want to move away and leave Alfred either.

As the mountain boy glanced over the dead trees toward where Ora Octavius had disappeared, D.J. stopped in his tracks.

"Now I remember!" he cried aloud.

Chapter Four

NAILS ABST COMES BACK TO TOWN

D.J. wanted to keep the gold nuggets with him, but he was afraid to take them to Sunday School. He hid them carefully in his room and dressed for church.

Snow had started gently falling when Dad turned the family sedan into the church parking lot. Almost every space was taken. There wasn't a family in town that hadn't been affected by the sudden closing of the town's major source of jobs. Judging by the crowded parking lot, everyone in town had gathered at church to soothe their troubled hearts.

D.J. could hardly wait to tell Alfred his latest news. D.J. saw his best friend standing by himself away from the little frame church with its corrugated roof and bell tower full of woodpecker holes. D.J. told his family he'd see them in church. He zipped up his jacket and hurried over to meet Alfred under a ponderosa away from everyone else.

"Guess what?" D.J. began.

Alfred looked as though he was trying to keep from crying. "Your father lost his job and you're going to move away."

D.J. blinked. "How'd you know?"

" 'Cause that's what we're going to have to do too!"

D.J. brightened. "Maybe we can all move close together!"

"That'd be great!" Alfred pulled his thick glasses off and used his handkerchief to wipe the melted snow from the lenses.

"Guess what else, Alfred?"

"What?"

"I think I saw the man who shouted at us and fired that thing at us!"

"You did? Where?"

Quickly, D.J. explained about meeting Ora Octavius. D.J. concluded, "I'm not sure, but I think it was the same voice."

"You know, D.J., we've just got to get to Indian Springs before he—or whoever—beats us to filing on that mine. I mean, if it can be claimed."

D.J. nodded. "I was thinking about that. We've got so much to do, but we'll have to be careful. Otherwise, people will get suspicious if we ask too many questions about old gold mines, and who owns the land, and how to file on a claim."

Alfred replaced his glasses and nodded. "Oh, I almost forgot! I looked up that little arrow in my reference books."

"What'd you find out?"

"It's a razor-tipped bolt fired from a powerful pistol crossbow. It's effective up to about sixty feet. And

it's every bit as deadly as a regular arrow. Of course,
it's quiet; there's no sound like a rifle to echo around
the mountains."

D.J. was thoughtful a moment. "That means whoever fired it was right on top of us! So he's a really
good woodsman! And we're risking terrible danger to
go back up there! But we've *got* to if we're going
back to the mine."

"We'd better go in; everyone else already has."

As the boys hurried across the newly-fallen snow,
D.J. glanced at the sky. "Maybe if this snow keeps
falling, they'll close school tomorrow. Dad'll
probably drive into Indian Springs to look for work
and we can ride with him."

Alfred raised his eyes past the shelter of the conifer
under which the boys stood. "Yeah! We need a snow
day* tomorrow! Come on, Snow! Keep falling!"

The little sanctuary was packed solid for church
services. Brother Paul rose like a giant Douglas fir*
against the twin windows in back of the pulpit and
opened his big black Bible.

"Brothers and sisters," he began soberly, looking
slowly around the packed pews at the glum faces,
"there's not a family here that's not hurting because
of the mill closing. But there's hope for you this
morning! We've got God's promise on that! So open
your Bibles first to the Old Testament."

D.J. heard the familiar rustle of thin pages
turning. He opened the Bible that had been his
mother's. His blue eyes skimmed the reference as
Brother Paul gave it: Proverbs, chapter three, verses
five and six.

"Trust in the Lord with all thine heart; and lean

not unto thine own understanding. In all thy ways
acknowledge Him, and He shall direct thy paths."

The lay pastor's big booming voice brought D.J.'s
eyes up from the page. "Now, keep your finger there in
the *King James Version* for a moment. Those of you
who have the paraphrased* *Living Bible* please turn
to First Corinthians, the third chapter and twenty-first
verse."

D.J. had the *King James Version,* but he turned to
the New Testament verse anyway. He read it quickly:
"Therefore let no man glory in men. For all things
are yours. . . . "

Brother Paul's voice interrupted the boy's reading.
"Now the *King James Version* says that we're not to
glory in men. That's not where it's at. So men, the
mill is not our source. God is! Now, let me read how
the paraphrased version puts that same sentence:
'God has already given you everything you need.' "

The words startled D.J. He stared at the lay
preacher while the thought burned itself into the boy's
mind. He automatically reached down to feel the
gold nuggets before remembering he had safely hidden
them behind his short stories in his bedroom. The
boy wanted to be an author someday, and nobody
touched the short stories he'd written.

Alfred nudged D.J. and whispered in his ear,
"That's true! God has already give us everything we
need! The mine! But nobody knows it except you
and me."

"Shh!" D.J. warned.

Brother Paul warmed up. His great arms swung
in wide circles. "You men who are suddenly out of
work this close to Christmas should not look at the

situation; at what it seems! God knows you've got to take care of your families—especially at this time of year—so He's given us words of hope. Let me read that paraphrase again: 'God has already given you everything you need.' "

The lay pastor's voice sank to a low rumble as it emerged from his big chest. "When you don't seem to have anything left, you've got the best of all: your faith in God's Word! So get in the Christmas spirit! Look up! We're going to celebrate Jesus' birthday! And He came that we might have life—and more abundantly at that! Believe it! I do!"

D.J. glanced around the tiny church. Slowly, as the booming voice of assurance rolled out like thunder from the pulpit, people's heads began to come up. The slump went from the shoulders of men and women alike. Old and young people raised their faces first to the pastor's and then looked through the two windows on either side of the homemade cross on the back wall behind Brother Paul. Snow was starting to stick to the evergreens outside the windows.

"It looks bad," Brother Paul cried, "but behind the clouds there's a sun that will shine again! Now I don't have any notion how God's going to work this out, but believe me—He will!"

After the service, people gathered in the front entry way to put on their coats and discuss the sermon. D.J. saw most were walking more briskly than when they had come into the church. They spoke cheerfully, having accepted the lay pastor's words as true.

D.J. heard Brother Dooley, an old man who had been a founder of the church, talking excitedly. "This

could be a tourist town! Lots of places around here
make lots of money off folks from San Francisco and
Sacramento and such! Why, we got scenery and
history and. . . . ”

D.J. didn't hear the rest. Alfred leaned over close
to whisper, "And a gold mine!"

"Watch it!" D.J. hissed warningly.

The boys pulled on their caps and jackets and
hurried out into the parking lot. Alfred let out a yell.

"Look how much snow's fallen! Tomorrow there'll
be no school and we can go to Indian Springs!"

D.J. grinned and bent impulsively to make a
snowball. He chased Alfred across the parking lot to
the curb where a black pickup loaded with firewood
was parked. Snow had not completely hidden the
chain saw, ax, mauls, gas can, and insulated cooler
with lunches that rested on top of the wood near the
cab.

The friends closed in a friendly scuffling match
that ended against the side of the truck.

As the boys were catching their breath, D.J.
nudged Alfred.

"Hey! There's Nails Abst! I forgot to tell you I saw
him in Stoney Ridge last night after I left you."

Both boys watched the town bully moving
through the snow, ducking his head down to keep the
snow from his eyes. The first time D.J. ever saw
Alfred was when he had recently arrived in Stoney
Ridge and Nails was threatening the skinny kid with
the thick glasses.

"Sure hope he's friendly," Alfred whispered.

Nails' too-big, badly scuffed boots made heavy
clumping sounds. Enough of his face showed above

the heavy jacket to disclose a down-turned mouth and damaged nose showing evidence of many fistfights. A pair of old striped overalls covered his lower body. His old winter coat was dirty and tattered.

"Hey, you two!" Nails yelled, raising his head about twenty feet from the boys. "Get away from my truck!"

D.J. shoved himself away from the vehicle as though he'd been leaning on a hot stove. "Sorry, Nails! I didn't realize it was yours! Haven't seen you in awhile!"

"Been cutting wood with my old man," Nails explained, coming close. D.J. caught a whiff of Nails' coat. It smelled like a wet dog.

Nails turned to glower at Alfred. "Well, Four Eyes, what're you looking at?"

"Nothing!" Alfred said, lowering his eyes. "I was surprised to see you. I thought you'd moved away."

"Well, I'm here! Now, get away from my truck!"

The two friends hurried through the snow toward their fathers' parked vehicles. Alfred muttered, "He sure doesn't seem to remember about your saving his life from the outlaw bear* that time. . . . "

D.J. interrupted. "Did you see inside the truck? On the front seat?"

"No, what?"

"I think I saw one of those things that shoots bolts. You know—like was fired at us!"

There was no way the boys could go back and check, but they looked at each other in surprise.

"But it wasn't Nails' voice yesterday," D.J. said thoughtfully. "I think it was that Ora Octavius fellow!"

"Could've been Nails' father's voice."

The boys considered. They weren't sure. They asked each other excited questions. Who had chased them on Jawbone Ridge? Had that person seen them find the gold? Was Nails' father mean enough to shoot a dart at them?

The boys parted without any answers, but a growing sense of urgency to get to the county seat.

*   *   *   *   *

Alfred was right about the snow day. Early Monday morning radio broadcasts from Indian Springs' only station announced the superintendent's telephoned message. This was a snow day. There was no school.

The Milfords didn't have a telephone, so Alfred's father called the Dillons from the pay phone in the little store near where the Milfords lived. Would Dad like to drive into Indian Springs and look for work with Alfred's father? Alfred was going, so D.J. could ride along and the boys could spend the day together.

D.J. dressed quickly, sliding the two heavy nuggets into his pocket. The weight against his leg gave him a good feeling.

Alfred and his father arrived in the used half-ton, four-wheel drive pickup with king cab that Mr. Milford had recently bought. The boys rode in the small space behind the two men. They followed the snow plows down to Indian Springs.

Since the county seat was fifteen hundred feet lower in elevation, there was only a dusting of snow on the steep streets of what had once been a gold rush community.

The boys made arrangements to meet their fathers for the ride home, then D.J. and Alfred excitedly hurried off, thinking what to do first.

"There're so many places to go!" D.J. exclaimed. "We've got to find out if we can file on that old mine, and who owns the land, and if there's a record of a claim—"

"Hey!" Alfred interrupted, pointing to an old Victorian house at the top of a steep hill on Main Street. "There's a place that sells mining equipment and buys gold! See the sign? Let's go in and find out how much the nuggets are worth!"

D.J. frowned. "The owner might be suspicious of kids like us having gold."

Alfred shook his head vigorously. "I know a couple of guys at school who make $30 or $40 some weekends panning gold from the river!"

"Well, OK—but don't let on where these came from."

"I promise!" Alfred said eagerly.

The friends pushed inside the warm store where a surprise was waiting.

Chapter Five

THE SECRET OF "CRAZY" CALHOUN

A sign over the counter read, *Gar Sanjen, Prop.*
Under that was a small blackboard with the chalked
notation: *Current Spot Price—$412.*

D.J. nudged Alfred as the boys made their way
through a half dozen tourists looking over mining
magazines, books on gold, and exhibits under glass
counters.

"Wonder if that price means per ounce?"

"Yes, but gold, like all precious metals, is weighed
in troy ounces rather than avoirdupois."*

D.J. shook his head, not understanding.

Alfred said, "Avoirdupois weight is based on the
16-ounce pound, but troy is based on 12-ounce
pounds."

Sometimes his best friend's knowledge bothered
D.J., who wanted to be a writer. Elmer Kersten, the
newspaper editor where D.J. worked as a stringer,*
had said a writer must know a lot about everything, or

43

at least know where to look it up. But D.J. had not yet developed the wide interests his writing would someday require.

While waiting for Mr. Sanjen, the boys looked around the various rooms in the old house that had been converted to a store. There were all kinds of mining equipment, ranging from pans and shovels to big dredges* the boys had often seen in the rivers.

In a semi-dark side room a portable television screen was playing a video cassette. It showed a young man in a black wet suit* demonstrating how to use a dredge to mine for gold flakes in rivers.

"What can I do for you boys?" Mr. Sanjen asked, coming up behind the friends.

The store owner looked like a tourist's version of a forty-niner. He wore a wide-brimmed leather hat, red shirt, red suspenders, and old blue jeans. His full beard was gray streaked with brown. He was a big, solidly built man whose fingers flashed six rings: three on each hand. Only his index fingers were bare. The rings were unique; obviously native nuggets mounted in massive settings.

D.J. delayed giving his real reason for being there. He pointed to a color photograph of a man's open palm pasted next to the cash register.

"Is that a gold nugget he's holding?"

"Sure is! Weighed fifteen troy ounces! Covers less than half his hand. One of my customers found it when he was digging a fire pit for his camp along a tributary of the Mad River."

"Wow!" Alfred exclaimed. "Let's see . . . based on the spot price on your board, times fifteen troy ounces . . . why, that's more than $6,000!"

"Would've been worth more than that if it wasn't such a flat blob," the gold dealer said. He tapped the color photograph and then pulled up a gold chain from around his neck until a nugget emerged from the front of his shirt.

"Now, this one's much smaller—only an inch and a half long—but it'll carry a premium because of its shape."

D.J. didn't think it looked like anything special until Mr. Sanjen said, "See? Looks like a kind of question mark."

"You buy much gold?" D.J. asked, still reluctant to bring out his nuggets.

"Quite a bit. Lots of people try their luck at placer mining* around here. You've probably seen them working the river outside of town. Even boys your age bring in a fair amount of dust and flakes."

D.J. asked, "How is gold bought?"

"Placer gold—like these little vials of gold flakes or these small nuggets under the counter—is immediately negotiable. It's sold for cash. But when people offer me gold coins or jewelry, I ask for a bill of sale so I don't buy stolen merchandise and maybe end up in jail on charges of being a fence.'"*

D.J. nodded, feeling the nuggets against his leg. "What'd you mean by *premium* nuggets?"

"Oh, something with special features. Sometimes the nugget resembles something: maybe the outline of a state or a president's profile. Things like that."

Alfred pushed up his thick glasses with his right thumb. "Then special shaped nuggets are worth more?"

"Yes; what we call 'spot plus.' That means the

current spot price plus ten, thirty, maybe forty or fifty percent more."

D.J. asked, "What about gold from a mine?"

"Only two kinds of gold around here; surface or free gold, like flakes and nuggets; called placer. That's usually found around or in rivers or creeks.

"The other kind of local gold is hard rock. It comes only from a deep mine. Most people wouldn't even recognize such quartz gold in a vein because it doesn't always look like gold.

"This piece is different." Mr. Sanjen opened the back of the glass counter and took out a pretty white rock about the size of a sugar cube. He set it on the counter.

"Gold in quartz like this is more rare these days. Hard rock or deep rock mining is too expensive. That's why, even with the price of gold as high as it is on the world market, it's not too common. When it was mined around here, the rock had to be crushed and the ore removed."

Alfred said, "My folks took me to the Empire Mine State Historic Park in Nevada County once. The docent* who showed us around explained all about how the gold was recovered from the rock."

Mr. Sanjen nodded and continued. "With the high waters and heavy snow melts we had this summer, more placer gold has been found around here than in years. But the deep rock mines are almost all closed. Some—like under this town—have a couple of hundred miles of tunnels now filled with water. Seeped in after the operators quit working the pumps a few decades back. That's when Cornish miners* had to work with hammers and drills deep underground."

D.J. felt his heart skip a beat at something the gold dealer had said. The boy touched the pretty white rock-like quartz. "Is that a vein of gold?" he asked.

"Part of one." The dealer put the quartz back and moved to a far corner of the counter. "You boys keep on talking if you want. I've got to finish up on this centrifugal force unit."

D.J. swallowed hard, following the man with Alfred. Something was troubling D.J. but he didn't know how to clarify it.

Alfred looked at the centrifugal force unit. It was about the size of a large bucket sitting on the counter.

"What's it do?" Alfred asked. "Spin the water around so fast it throws out everything into the center drain and leaves the heavier gold? Is that what's left in the black sand or whatever I see still in the bottom?"

"That's right. The centrifugal force works everything off but the heavy black sand. Then I work that down to see if there are any gold flakes. See? I've got a whole bucket of those heavy materials that came off a dredge or sluicing. Maybe you saw that part done on the video screen?"

The boys nodded as Mr. Sanjen used a large shallow dipper to lift black sand from a bucket into a washtub of water.

D.J.'s troubled mind had framed his thoughts carefully. He asked, "Are you saying that placer gold and quartz gold aren't found together?"

"Quartz comes from deep underground while placer is found on the surface. It's not the same thing."

For the first time, Alfred seemed to realize what D.J. was thinking. The boys' eyes met as they considered a strange discovery.

D.J. made up his mind. He reached into his pocket and pulled out the nuggets.

Mr. Sanjen's eyes widened. "What've you got there?"

"I found them," D.J. said softly. "One's shaped like a heart; the other like—"

The dealer interrupted. "Sometimes I pay two or three times the market value for nuggets with distinctive features. Want me to weigh those for you?"

D.J. nodded and followed the dealer to a small set of balance scales. He carefully lifted the larger nugget from D.J.'s palm and placed it on one end of the scales. He took some weights from another box. D.J. noticed each weight was stamped *Troy*.

When the delicate scales were perfectly balanced, Mr. Sanjen bent and looked carefully. "Five ounces. Nearly half a pound! Now, let's try the other one."

It balanced out at three ounces.

"Give you top dollar for them," the dealer said, standing up straight again. "This close to Christmas, I'll be able to sell them pretty fast, I think. So I'll give more than I might in the summertime."

D.J. shook his head and put both nuggets back in his pocket. "No, thanks. They're not for sale—at least, not now."

Outside the store, Alfred was almost jumping up and down. "Do you realize how much those are worth, D.J.? Spot price plus premium. . . . "

"Shh!" D.J. hissed, looking around at the tourists and Christmas shoppers. "Somebody'll *hear* you!"

"So what? Mr. Sanjen knows—"

"He doesn't know who we are!" D.J. interrupted.

"But what worries me is that my nuggets couldn't have come from that mine!"

"How do you explain that, D.J.?"

"I don't know. This gets more complicated all the time! Come on! Let's get to the courthouse and see what we have to do to find out if we can file on that mine."

The boys hurried up the hilly streets of Indian Springs. Alfred dodged a woman and two small children. He said softly, "We've got to protect ourselves, D.J.! We've got to keep our gold safe!"

D.J. felt a tinge of annoyance as he had earlier. Alfred hadn't found the gold; D.J. had, but his friend sounded as though they were equal finders. D.J. tried not to think about that just now.

The boys were passing the local newspaper office on the way to the courthouse when D.J. had a sudden idea. He clutched Alfred's coat sleeve and spun him out of the pedestrian traffic.

"Editors know everything! Let's ask Mr. Kersten, but we've got to be careful what we say!"

Elmer Kersten owned the county weekly newspaper where D.J. was a stringer. Mr. Kersten also belonged to the county historical society. He often ran articles about the old days when gold and timber had attracted the first settlers to what was now Timbergold County.

The editor's office was small, cramped, and untidy. Mr. Kersten sat before an ancient rolltop desk staggering under stacks of papers, letters, newspapers, and just plain junk.

The editor was a tall man with shoulders stooped from many years of leaning over a typewriter. He

was bald except for a rim of pure white hair which
ran around the back of his head and above his ears.
His large stomach extended beyond his belt in what
D.J.'s grandfather called a "dunlop, because it done
lopped over."

D.J. perched on the straight-backed visitor's chair
while Alfred leaned against one of the many old
wooden filing cabinets. These were near the two
radio receivers tuned down so they were barely
audible. One was tuned to the county sheriff's band
and the other radio was tuned to the state highway
patrol frequency.

Mr. Kersten swiveled in his old chair. It squeaked
like an animal in pain.

"D.J., I'm glad you came by! Been planning to call
you. All my regular people are busy with Christmas
stories. But there've been so many complaints about
firewood ripoffs that—"

"Firewood ripoffs?" D.J. interrupted.

"Very common this time of year, D.J. Some
firewood sellers are cheating customers. Like charging
for a cord* and delivering less, hiding poor wood
under a layer of good wood on their trucks, and so
forth.

"As a stringer, D.J., you could check out that story.
Interview Clivus Bushrod at the Timbergold County
Department of Weights and Measures. Write
something like Tips for the Consumer. Be sure to let
Clivus see the piece before you turn it in. Can't be too
careful about accuracy, you know."

D.J. squirmed a little uncomfortably. That
assignment didn't interest him at all. "Well, OK, Mr.
Kersten, I'll do that. But I'd like to ask you something

else first."

"Oh? What?"

"Yeah!" Alfred broke in eagerly. "D.J.'d like to do some writing about old mines and things. Are there any legends about lost gold mines around here?"

Mr. Kersten laughed. "Now boys, newspaper editors are downright suspicious of just about everybody and everything. You want to go looking for the local version of the Lost Dutchman,* the Gunsight, or the Breyfogel—right?"

He leaned forward, not waiting for an answer.

"Well, let me set your minds at rest. None of those famous lost mines is in this area. In Timbergold County, every claim worth anything has been registered over at the courthouse. Sorry, boys, but there are no lost mines around here."

The boys' faces fell. They fidgeted uneasily, feeling their hopes crushed.

"Unless . . . " Mr. Kersten said thoughtfully, frowning and reaching for the stack of papers on his desk. He rummaged through them, sending some flying onto the floor.

"Unless what?" D.J. prompted, picking up the papers and putting them back on the untidy stack.

The editor pulled a very old hardcover book from somewhere in the mess and began flipping through it. "Unless you count the stories about 'Crazy' Calhoun," the editor said. "He died about 75 years ago. He was a loner, always out prospecting by himself, just as some people still do today. But one day Calhoun showed up with some of the richest quartz gold anybody had ever seen. Wouldn't tell anybody where he found it, of course. Just said he'd struck it rich in a mine."

"What happened?" D.J. asked, thinking he might have discovered the old prospector's mine.

"Well, nobody ever did find where Calhoun really got his gold, and those who tried to follow him to the mine came back with wild stories about spooky things happening to them."

D.J. could hardly breathe he was so excited. "Where was the mine supposed to be?"

"Nobody rightly knows, except somewhere around Jawbone Ridge. Anyway, Calhoun finally just vanished. His secret went with him. About the only thing folks know for sure is that Calhoun used to say the mine was cursed."

"Cursed?" The boys spoke as one and reached for the old book. The editor didn't seem to notice and continued holding it.

"Well, not really *cursed,* of course; there's no such thing, except what we read about in the Bible. But there's one story—it's in this old book—about the mine having some kind of mystery to it."

"What was the mystery?" D.J. asked breathlessly.

"As I remember, Calhoun claimed that once a few men did manage to follow him to the mine. They tied him up and entered the shaft. But they all died— some mysterious and invisible germ or gas or something—got everyone except Calhoun."

Alfred nodded. "Probably methane gas. Comes from rotting vegetation—even old timbers. Has no odor or color, yet it's poisonous and explosive."

The editor nodded. "You must read a lot, Alfred. Methane's *really* deadly." He paused. "You boys aren't thinking of going into some old mines, are you?

They're very, very dangerous—you could be trapped
by a cave-in, or be overcome by deadly fumes, or
you could end up getting lost in the tunnels. You two
should stay out of such places!"

Before the boys could answer, the editor stopped
turning pages. "Ah! Here it is! The chapter called,
'Mystery of the Black Hole Mine.' "

Both boys said together, " 'The Black Hole
Mine'?" They leaned forward to gaze at the page.

Mr. Kersten added, "That's what Calhoun called
it. But remember, everybody pretty much believed the
old man made up the whole thing. Of course, he did
show up with some rich quartz gold. Anyway, if the
mine ever did exist, its location is lost to history.

"Calhoun never filed a claim on it, so it'd belong
to whoever found it. I've heard that some of those old
recluses up in the hills sometimes look for it. But no
sensible person does. It just doesn't exist."

D.J. wasn't so sure. He asked if he could borrow
the book. Mr. Kersten handed it to D.J. and told him to
have the firewood ripoff story finished for next
week's edition.

D.J. carried the borrowed book to the street. As
soon as the boys turned the corner, they stopped and
examined the book. The friends quickly read the
short article.

Their eyes met. "No doubt about it," D.J.
whispered. "I've rediscovered the Black Hole Mine!"

"Yeah," Alfred whispered back. His Adam's apple
worked up and down in his skinny throat as though he
were having trouble breathing. "But what else have
we done?"

Chapter Six

CHASED BY SHADOWS

The boys hurried across town and began climbing the steep hill to the courthouse. It was the original three-story brown brick building erected in the 1850s and infrequently modified. A white Statue of Justice stood over the front entrance above the high concrete steps. At the building's center, a golden dome capped the highest point. This was above a fancy tiered section that looked like the decoration from a giant wedding cake except there was no bride and groom, only the gilded ball.

Alfred complained, "Everything in Indian Springs is either straight up or straight down, and we always have to go where it's straight up."

"Climbing these hills will keep you in shape for going back to the mine."

"Hey! Look! Nails' truck is parked up ahead."

Both boys glanced nervously around, but neither Nails nor his father was in sight.

"Let's peek inside the cab and see if that crossbow's there," D.J. said.

The friends carefully approached the black pickup. Being mountain boys, D.J. and Alfred recognized it as a half-ton model with a 380 cubic inch engine. The original factory long pickup bed had been replaced with a flatbed and stake sides so it would hold stacked wood. The truck probably had overload springs because hardwood is heavy.

Tinsley Abst had failed to cut his front wheels against the curb to prevent a possible runaway vehicle. He could get a traffic ticket for unsafe parking.

"Can you see inside yet?" Alfred asked as the boys neared the truck.

"Another minute . . . oh! Mr. Abst is coming out of the courthouse!"

"Should we cross the street?"

"No. That'd look funny. Keep your head down and keep walking. Maybe he won't recognize us."

Tinsley Abst was a professional bear hunter who had originally come to Stoney Ridge to take an outlaw bear on which there was a big bounty. Apparently, he also cut firewood for added income.

Nails' father was a big man with heavy unshaven jaws covered with black stubble. His face was flushed with anger and he was muttering to himself. Both boys silently stepped aside and let the man pass down the street toward his truck.

"Whew!" Alfred said when the pickup's door opened and slammed. "Glad he didn't recognize us! Wonder what he's so mad about?"

D.J. shrugged. "Just so it's not us. Well, let's go in to the recorder-clerk's office and see who owns that land. Then we'll have to find out how to file a claim—if that mine isn't already owned by someone."

They entered the ancient courthouse which had the faintly-unpleasant smell of old buildings. The boys found the county recorder and clerk's office on the second floor. Samuel Ging was a nice-looking man about the same age as Sam Dillon. He leaned across the counter. "What can I do for you, boys?"

D.J. asked, "How do we find out who owns a particular piece of land?"

"Depends on where it is. In town or some of the incorporated areas, we've got the records. But if it's public land, like B.L.M. or U.S.D.A–Forest Service, sometimes called U.S.F.S., then you'll have to see them."

"B.L.M.?" D.J. asked.

"Bureau of Land Management and U.S. Forest Service. The latter's under the Department of Food and Agriculture. Public lands are administered through federal offices. The Forestry Service is at the edge of town, but B.L.M.'s in Sacramento. If you're talking about property out in these mountains, you're in the wrong department."

D.J. looked at Alfred. Both boys knew that Jawbone Ridge was public land. They thanked the recorder-clerk and walked back into the echoing hallway.

"We may as well check on the firewood story while we're here," D.J. said. "I hate to take the time, but it's better to get it done."

"Keep it short," Alfred urged. "We've got to find out if we can file on that land."

The boys found the Department of Weights and

Measures in a cramped corner of the third story.
They introduced themselves to Clivus Bushrod and explained Elmer Kersten's idea for a firewood ripoff
story.

Mr. Bushrod was a thin man with black horn-
rimmed glasses. He was totally bald on the front half of
his head except for one small brown patch in the
middle of his scalp.

"Glad to get a little publicity on that score, boys,"
he said. He walked to the end of the counter and tipped
up the hinged end. "In fact, right now I'm glad to see
a friendly face. A few minutes ago I was royally
chewed out by an irate woodcutter."

Mr. Bushrod motioned the boys through the
counter opening. They followed him to a desk that had
probably once been army surplus.* They sat down
as their host lowered his thin body into the armchair
behind the desk.

D.J. began, "I never thought about it before Mr.
Kersten suggested the story, but in a county like this
where almost everyone burns wood for heating, I
guess firewood ripoffs are a big problem."

"Sure are!" Mr. Bushrod began. He pushed his
glasses up on top of his bald pate. "Each household
burns from one to six cords of wood per winter.
Figure about three cords as an average. This is usually
bought from an itinerant* firewood seller.

"We don't require a license except to sell inside
the city limits. Most of these woodcutters are honest,
but some are not. Most don't follow state law,
especially in failing to give a receipt. The seller can be
prosecuted for not offering one. You'd be amazed
how many people buy firewood without any idea of the

seller's name and address, yet they want our office to prosecute the seller for some fraudulent act."

D.J. began making notes on the sheet of paper Mr. Kersten had taught the boy to always have handy.

"But," Mr. Bushrod continued, "not all the angry people are victims. As I mentioned, I just had a very angry woodcutter in here bawling me out."

D.J. and Alfred exchanged glances. "Tinsley Abst?" D.J. asked aloud, looking at the man across the desk.

"You know him? A hard case! I've had so many complaints against him! Some went to the district attorney for prosecution."

D.J. frowned. "What'd he do?"

"A better question might be, 'What didn't he do?' He's been cutting wood up on Jawbone Ridge—"

"Jawbone Ridge?" both boys exclaimed together.

"Yes, but he had permission, so that's not the issue. I've had complaints about him delivering short loads but charging for a full cord, failing to give a receipt as required by law—that sort of thing. Then he got mad at me when I tried to explain what the law requires."

D.J. hadn't been interested in the firewood assignment, but knowing Nails and his father had been on Jawbone Ridge made a big difference. D.J. leaned forward and listened carefully till Mr. Bushrod finished explaining everything.

"I'll tell all the readers in a story," D.J. assured him, glancing at his notes. "I mean about inspecting the load for size, soundness, and dryness before the buyer allows the wood to be off-loaded from the truck."

"Don't forget to make sure it's a full cord, D.J. Remember, the only legal way to sell wood is in cords or portions of cords. And a cord is 128 cubic feet, well stowed and packed. That's what the law requires."

D.J. stood up. "Well, guess that's enough for now. I'll type this up and bring it in for you to check before it's printed."

The boys went down the courthouse steps together. Alfred mused, "Taking what Mr. Bushrod said about everyone in this county buying from one to six cords of wood a winter, and paying between $100 and $150 a cord . . . that's a lot of money!"

"Sure is," D.J. replied, "but I'm more interested in learning who owns that land where we found . . . you know . . . and what the requirements are to file."

"Are we headed for the forestry service?"

"Library's on the way. Let's take a minute and check out any books we can find on the history of gold mining in this area."

D.J. took a shortcut behind long, narrow brick buildings with iron shutters that had stood since the Gold Rush of 1849. The boys approached the library which was much newer. It had been built around the time of World War I.

The friends climbed the few steep concrete steps and entered the building. They removed their coats and caps and left them on chairs by a table before going into the stacks. The library was too hot, but apparently the staff kept it that way for the many older people who sat at different tables and read or talked quietly.

D.J. whispered, "Here's the section. You look

through that shelf and I'll take the bottom one."

Alfred nodded and sat down on a small metal footstool with wheels. D.J. sat on the floor beside him and began pulling books off the shelf.

"Not much here," he whispered after awhile. "Just stuff about all the mines everybody knows about."

"Maybe the only book we're going to have is this one that the newspaper editor loaned us, but let's take all we can. Might find something interesting in one of them."

The boys finally pulled out the maximum number of books each could check out on his library card. As they headed down the narrow aisle between the high stacks to check out, D.J. heard a man's voice through the stack on his right.

"You work here, Miss? Where'll I find the section on local gold mines?"

D.J. grabbed at Alfred's sleeve so quickly he knocked a book out of his friend's hand.

"Hey!" Alfred whispered in surprise. "What'd you do that for?" He bent to pick up the book.

D.J. quickly drew Alfred a few steps down the nearest side aisle in the stacks. D.J. whispered, "Did you hear that?"

"Hear what?"

"That voice in the next aisle! Recognize it?"

"I wasn't listening. Why?"

"It's *him!*" D.J. hissed. "The voice we heard threatening us in the woods! The one who fired the bolt!"

"I thought Tinsley Abst did that."

"Maybe—or maybe it was somebody else. We don't know for sure. I don't remember any of their

voices that well. But I'm *sure* that whoever's over in
that stack of books is the same one who yelled at us!
We've got to get a look at him!"

The boys circled the stacks and tried to relocate
the man, but they didn't see anyone except the usual
elderly men and women. D.J. had an idea.

"Let's check out these books and wait outside. He
should be easy to recognize because his voice says he's
much younger than anybody else in here."

As the boys hurried to the checkout desk, Alfred
whispered, "You think he followed us here?"

"I don't know! But we've got to get a good look at
him! I don't like being chased by shadows!"

Alfred handed over his library card at the desk
and the librarian stamped it. But D.J. was nervous,
anxiously watching to see if the unknown man came
out of the stacks before D.J. checked out his book. The
man would recognize them, but the boys didn't
know anything about him except the sound of his
voice.

In his hurry, D.J. pulled his library card out of his
pocket too fast. The smaller nugget came with it. The
gold landed heavily at the boys' feet.

He instantly bent and scooped it up. D.J. glanced
around as he straightened quickly, the nugget safely in
his hand. Nobody had even looked up from reading.

But Alfred cleared his throat warningly and
jerked his head toward the stacks. D.J.'s eyes shot
there. Through a hole between the books, the boy
saw only a man's eyes.

Alfred whispered, "He saw it before you picked it
up."

"You sure?"

"I'm sure!"

"Did you get a good look at him?"

"No!"

The librarian stamped D.J.'s card and returned it to him. The boy grabbed it and his books.

"Come on!" he whispered. "Let's get out of here!"

They tried to appear casual as they retrieved their coats and caps to walk out the door. Outside, they hurried down the high concrete steps and ran to the corner. They raced across the street and stood facing the old library with its high windows.

"D.J., I'm scared," Alfred said. He shivered in the crisp November air. "Why don't we get out of here before something terrible happens to us?"

"He can't hurt us here in town. Besides, we've *got* to see what he looks like. The door's opening! Maybe that's him!"

Chapter Seven

SHARP WORDS BETWEEN FRIENDS

D.J. held his breath as two older women came through the front door of the library. The boy anxiously looked behind the women. But nobody else came out the door.

Alfred suddenly gripped his friend's sleeve. "Hey, look!" He pointed across the street. "The library window just to the left of the door!"

D.J. saw the venetian blind settle into place.

"He was watching us!" D.J. breathed. "Did you get a look at him?"

Alfred shook his head. "No! I just saw the blinds move and caught a glimpse of a man's face. He must have seen me point and dropped the blind!"

"He'll probably try to go out another way so we can't see him. You stay here—I'll take the back door."

D.J. sprinted to the crosswalk and down to the alley behind the library. He ran to where he could see the back door. There he pressed himself against the rough side of an old brick building and waited.

If the man came out that way, D.J. planned to duck back quickly so he wouldn't be seen. But first he'd get a good look at the man.

The minutes dragged by, but the library's back door remained closed. The early December cold seeped through the boy's still form and he shivered. He stared at the library door till tiny flecks of light seemed to dance in the air, but nobody came out.

A hand touched D.J.'s shoulder from behind. He spun, automatically crouching and bringing up his hands to defend himself.

"Alfred! You scared me half to death!"

"You scared me too when you didn't come back! I finally went inside and checked every aisle. He's not in there, D.J."

"I'd sure like to know who he is!" D.J. was highly frustrated, but his friend was not so concerned.

Alfred shrugged, "Oh, well—guess we'd better hurry to the forestry department before we have to meet our dads."

The boys zigzagged across town, alternatingly jogging and walking. They came to a long, low, one-story green building near the edge of town. D.J. led the way through the front door under the sign, *U.S. Department of Forestry.*

Moments later, the boys were talking to a middle-aged man with a small neat mustache and wavy brown hair.

"I'm Bill Haskins, realty officer dealing with lands and mining. What can I do for you boys?"

D.J. repeated his reason for being there. The man led them to a brown leatherette sofa away from the counter and motioned them to sit. He sat in a small green plastic chair, facing them.

D.J. took out his folded note paper and pencil. "Mr. Haskins, can people still file on gold mine claims today?"

"Sure, D.J. You've probably seen lots of amateur gold miners panning along Mad River or its tributaries. Probably seen men in wet suits working dredges and other placer mining equipment?"

Both boys nodded. Such scenes were fairly common in the foothills of the Mother Lode country around Indian Springs. Such mining was rarer 1,500 feet higher where D.J. and Alfred lived.

"Well, boys, today gold mining is more scientific, of course. It's usually done in three stages: prospecting, exploration, and development."

As D.J.'s pencil skimmed along his note pad, Alfred asked, "Prospecting means looking for gold, I guess. But what are the other two?"

"Exploration means what you do after finding 'color.' You know—gold flakes in the pan or dredge which is used to recover the gold."

"What about a mine?" Alfred asked impulsively.

D.J. stopped writing and gave his friend a warning look.

Mr. Haskins didn't seem to notice. "Expensive hard rock mining is much rarer than placer mining, of course. But there are definite steps a hard rock miner would have to take."

"Such as?" D.J. prompted.

"See that map on the wall over there?" Both boys' eyes followed the man's pointing finger. "That's color-coded to show who owns the land. Green is ours;

forestry land. We're under the U.S. Department of Agriculture. Yellow is controlled by the Bureau of Land Management. White is private, pink is military, and blue is either water—like lakes—or state-owned. So the first thing someone has to do when filing a claim is to determine who owns the land."

Alfred got up and approached the map. He stood very close to it, his thick glasses and nose almost against the paper.

D.J. turned to Mr. Haskins. "You're saying it's hard to file a gold claim?"

"No, not really. There are just steps one has to take. Like seeing the county recorder, filing a notice of intent, and if it's a big operation—like a deep rock mine—a plan of operation must be filed."

D.J. felt discouragement at all that was involved. He looked up as Alfred came back and sat down.

Alfred whispered, "Yellow."

Even though the word was spoken softly, Mr. Haskins caught it. "If you're interested in a claim on B.L.M. land, you'd have to go to their office in Sacramento."

D.J. felt his discouragement rising, so he heard only snatches of what Mr. Haskins was saying. " . . . file a legal description. Stake the claim. See how much value there is. Maybe hire a geologist to advise. Take samples by drilling, have it assayed, then zero in on the best location.

"After exploration comes the development. The claimant could try working the claim himself, but he'd need to crush it if it's hard rock, and find a way to reclaim the ore. Or he could sell shares or even sell outright to a bigger company because it takes knowledge, money, and equipment to develop a claim."

D.J. shook his head. All that was impossible! He made a few more notes to be polite, then thanked Mr. Haskins and left with Alfred.

Heading back toward downtown Indian Springs, D.J. cried out. "There's *no way* I can do all those things! It'll take tons of money."

Alfred pushed his thick glasses up with his gloved right thumb. "You know, D.J., we still don't have this thing straightened out. Something is very mixed up."

"You mean because I found surface or placer gold nuggets where there's a hard rock mine. From what we've learned, that isn't logical! Those two kinds of gold just aren't found together!"

"Then what does it mean, D.J.?"

"The kids at school call you 'The Brain,' so why don't you tell me?"

"You *know* I hate that name, D.J.!"

"I don't mean it the way they do, Alfred! But I'm stumped, and unless you can figure it out, there's only one thing we can do."

Alfred shook his head. "If you're thinking of going back up there—remember what the guy said when he fired that bolt at us."

"It's the only way, Alfred! And it's worth the risk!"

Alfred groaned. "Aw, D.J.!"

"We've got no choice, Alfred! Our fathers are out of work! It's nearly Christmas, and the only thing I've got going is this mine!"

Alfred mused, "Even if the guy with the dart doesn't get us, the mine might. You heard what Mr. Kersten said about all those terrible things that happened to people who entered the mine!"

"Just stories, Alfred! Wild stories told by a crazy old prospector to scare people away from his claim!"

Alfred sagged against a lamppost. "Maybe—maybe not. Suppose we get up there and something terrible happens to us?"

"Nothing'll happen!" D.J. scoffed.

His friend sadly shook his head. "D.J., I know you like to explore and have adventures, but since we found that gold, you've been acting—"

D.J. exploded, "Stop saying *we* and *our*. *You* didn't find those nuggets! *I* did!"

For a second, Alfred blinked in surprise but said nothing. Finally he protested softly, "There's no need to bite my head off, D.J.! We were together when it happened, and we've always shared—"

"Not the gold!" D.J. interrupted again. He was surprised to hear himself say that.

Alfred said softly, "I see. It's OK for me to take the risks with you, but not to share in the gold. D.J., that's not like you!"

D.J. took a short breath to gain control of his emotions. "I'm sorry, Alfred. It's just that things are getting so mixed up, I don't know what to think."

"Except you're thinking that maybe those two nuggets are all we're going to find."

"I said, 'Stop saying—' " D.J. caught himself and snapped his mouth shut so hard his teeth clicked.

Alfred looked at D.J. a long time without saying anything. Then he walked silently up the street.

D.J. called, "Where are you going?"

Alfred didn't stop or turn around. "To try finding my best friend. I haven't seen him for a while!"

Chapter Eight

A SECOND SHARP DISAGREEMENT

For a moment, D.J. stared after his friend. In all the time the boys had known each other, they'd never had a cross word. D.J. was surprised at how he felt about the gold. He had never before felt anything that came close to greed, coveting, or even much selfishness. Yet somehow the desire for the gold was strange and powerful, making D.J. say and do things so unlike him.

Slowly he followed his friend back toward where their fathers had agreed to meet them. As D.J. walked, he imagined himself entering the lost mine and finding gold everywhere. Nuggets lay around like marbles, ready to be picked up. Then his thoughts jumped. Nuggets weren't found in hard rock passageways. He imagined reaching for a vein of quartz where the gold ran like a golden thread, but the gold vanished.

D.J. shook his head to drive away the thought.

Well, if he found lots of gold he'd give some to Alfred. Maybe not, though. Sharing gold wasn't like dividing candy, an apple, or an orange.

Of course, it would be different with his family, D.J. thought. He'd give them everything they needed, and Dad wouldn't even have to work anymore. So it didn't matter if the mill was closed. Maybe D.J. would even hire all the unemployed lumber workers in Stoney Ridge to work his mine. Maybe he'd even need to hire people from Indian Springs!

Or maybe, he told himself sadly, *it'll turn out to be a big nothing and there won't be any more gold!"*

As he passed a hardware store, he stopped to look through the window at some items displayed there. Maybe for Christmas he'd get Dad one of those electric saws so he could make things in the garage. Two Mom would like—

The boy's thoughts were snapped off when he caught a sudden movement reflected in the glass window. Lots of people were going up and down the street under the Christmas decorations. Yet D.J.'s sharp eyes, trained to spot wild creatures moving quietly in the woods, caught something unusual. A man across the street and some distance back had suddenly turned into an alley.

The boy whirled around, but the man was gone. D.J. frowned, wondering. Had he just seen some innocent person changing his mind and ducking down the alley as a shortcut to somewhere? Or had somebody been following Alfred and him— somebody who didn't want to be seen?

D.J. felt goosebumps crinkle the skin on his forearms. He ran to catch up with Alfred, ignoring the strained relationship between them. "I think somebody's following us!" D.J. said.

Alfred replied promptly, seemingly anxious to forget the little tiff they had just had. "Oh? Who?"

"I don't know." D.J. quickly explained about the suspicious man he'd seen reflected in the store window.

Alfred pushed his thick glasses up with an automatic thrust of his right thumb. "Think he'll try to follow us home? Find out where we live?"

D.J. pursed his lips thoughtfully. "He might. But darkness comes so early he might not be able to do it. Tail lights in these twisting mountain roads would be hard to follow back to Stoney Ridge."

"But he might be able to do it," Alfred insisted. "D.J., I don't mind telling you it's spooky having these things happen since we—you—found the—you know." Alfred glanced around anxiously.

The boys walked on together, talking to ease the tension that had sprung up between them a short time before.

"You know, Alfred, since Jawbone Ridge is on B.L.M. land and I'd have to go to Sacramento to find out about filing on the claim, I'd better be sure there's really gold in that mine."

Alfred stopped dead still in the sidewalk so a woman with an armload of packages almost bumped into him.

"You mean—go past the place where the dart was fired at us and into the mine itself?"

"It's the *only* way, Alfred. I've got to know for sure what's there! I mean—if we found nuggets and that's not what comes from an underground mine—"

Alfred interrupted fiercely. "You heard what the editor said! Old mines are *dangerous!*"

"It's worth the risk, Alfred!"

"Maybe—if there's gold! But if it turns out that you've already found all there is, and you go down into that old spooky mine alone—"

D.J. broke in. "You could come with me!"

"No way!" Alfred shook his head so hard his glasses almost flew off his head.

"Then I'll go by myself!" D.J. said firmly.

"You're not talking like yourself, D.J.! Maybe you've got gold fever or something! Whatever you do, don't do *that!*" Alfred's voice rose sharply.

"Shh!" D.J. cautioned as the boys neared their fathers waiting in a free city parking lot. "Our dads will hear us!"

"Maybe they should!" Alfred said defiantly. "What you're planning is dangerous!"

"You promised!" D.J. hissed. "You can't tell anyone!"

"I only promised about the nuggets—not about some dumb thing like going into the mine!"

"It's the same thing, Alfred!"

"No, it's not! What if something happens to you?"

"Nothing's going to happen! Besides, I'm doing it for my family!"

Alfred's right hand came up in an automatic movement. He pushed the thick glasses up higher on the bridge of his nose before asking softly, "Are you, D.J.?"

For a moment, D.J. gazed thoughtfully at his friend. "If you won't go in with me, you can't have any of the gold!"

"I haven't gotten any so far, anyway."

D.J. abruptly walked away from Alfred. D.J. knew he shouldn't be angry with his best friend, but D.J. was, and he tried to tell himself he was justified.

He told himself fiercely, *It'll be mine alone! And why shouldn't it be? I found it. If Alfred would go into the mine with me and help, he could have some gold. But if I have to take all the risks myself—no!*

Their second sharp disagreement caused a strained silence to settle over both boys on the drive home. Their fathers didn't seem to notice. Their quietness told the boys what they needed to know: neither man had found work or any hopeful signs.

It was almost painful for D.J. to sit beside his best friend in the backseat of the king cab pickup and not talk. D.J. tried to think of other things.

He remembered the man's reflection in the store window. The boy glanced back from time to time as their truck started climbing toward Stoney Ridge. Mr. Milford drove slowly, his headlights on against the early darkness. Some cars passed in the few turnouts* on the narrow mountain road. They were climbing back to the snowline. Dirty snow reflected the headlights back from the sides of the road. Evergreen trees glistened on the hillside. D.J.'s ears popped from the change in altitude.

After awhile he thought one car's headlights kept well behind the Milford vehicle, neither gaining nor falling behind. When Alfred's father turned off the state highway onto the surface streets of Stoney Ridge, D.J. felt sure there was a car following them.

Ordinarily, he'd have shared this thought with Alfred. But D.J. didn't feel like talking.

It was full dark when Mr. Milford pulled up in front of D.J.'s home. D.J. felt miserable because of the disagreement with his friend. To ease his misery, D.J. told himself he had a right to be angry with Alfred. Deep inside himself, D.J. knew he wasn't behaving properly. It wasn't Christian; D.J. knew that, but he didn't allow himself to dwell on that thought.

The boys exchanged polite, reserved "good nights" and parted with their personal problem unresolved.

As the Milfords drove away, D.J. saw a pair of headlights come on about two blocks away.

Coincidence? D.J. followed his father from the sidewalk to the front steps. When Dad opened the door, D.J. saw the car come even with the Dillon house. The boy tried to see inside the darkened vehicle, but it was useless. D.J. didn't recognize the sedan. It climbed steadily on up the hill the way the Milfords had driven. D.J. went inside without being sure whether somebody had followed him home or not.

The boy felt tension growing inside. Nothing was going right; in fact, everything seemed to be getting worse.

Two Mom had supper ready. After Pris asked the blessing, Two Mom started passing the steaming dishes.

"Well," she said cheerfully, "just because the Lord didn't provide a job right away doesn't mean anything. Tomorrow's another day! So right after the dishes are washed, let's put up Christmas decorations."

Pris' mop of wild brown hair bobbed as she looked up sharply from her plate. "We don't have a tree yet!"

"We'll do without this year," Two Mom said quietly. "We'll decorate the rest of the house."

"Mom, we could cut down one of the wild trees. There are zillions of them on every hill around here!"

"It's against the law, Pris. There are only certain places where you can cut trees, and you need a permit. So we'll just do without a Christmas tree this year. D.J., you can help with the ladder to get tinsel around the ceiling light fixture."

"I don't feel like putting decorations up tonight," D.J. answered softly. He reluctantly took a scoop of brussels sprouts because Two Mom had a three bite rule. Everyone had to eat three mouthfuls of everything, even if the family member hated that particular food.

"It'll be fun!" Two Mom insisted. She passed seconds of freshly-baked buns around in a wicker basket. "Won't it, Priscilla?"

"I made something at school," the nine-year-old stepsister said brightly. "It's a surprise! Could I put it up first? In the front window?"

"Why not?" Two Mom said. "D.J., since this is our first Christmas as a family, do you have a favorite decoration or something?"

The boy poured white vinegar over the hated brussels sprouts. He'd have preferred mayonnaise, but his stepmother had strict ideas of nutrition. "I've got a little tree I made in the first grade. Mom always . . . "

His voice trailed off, thinking about his dead mother.

Two Mom seemed to understand. She said cheerfully, "I like the manger scene best. It makes me think how the real one must have been that night so long ago in Bethlehem. Sam, what's your favorite?"

Dad didn't answer. He chewed in silence, his eyes on the dish of red beans before him.

Two Mom tried again. "Sam, it's always hard to be the father in a time like this. But our heavenly Father cares, just as you do. He'll—"

Dad interrupted sharply. "I *know* that, Hannah! But until some money comes into this house again, I'm going to be a little uptight! OK?"

Two Mom replied softly, "I wasn't going to say anything just now, but when Pris and I walked downtown today, I learned there's a part-time waitress job open."

Pris let out a loud wail. "I don't want you to go to work again! You promised when you got married to Dad Dillon you'd stay home!"

Two Mom reached out with her left hand and squeezed her daughter's forearm. "It may be necessary for awhile, Pris. We all have to do what we can sometimes—like now."

D.J. nodded thoughtfully. *That's right,* he told himself with fresh resolve. *And I've got to go check out that mine! Then I'll know if we're rich or not.*

He tried not to think about the dangers waiting for him back up on Jawbone Ridge.

Chapter Nine

DAD CLAMPS DOWN

It was still dark the next morning when Dad pounded on D.J.'s door. D.J. awakened and sat on the edge of his bed with mixed emotions. He had a heavy, sick feeling inside because of his disagreement with Alfred.

D.J. was also concerned about the family having no money for Christmas. Then there was the uncertainty of whether somebody had followed him yesterday. And what would happen when he went back up on Jawbone Ridge and entered the Black Hole Mine?

It certainly didn't feel like three weeks before Christmas, the most joyous time of the year!

The local radio broadcaster announced that the roads had been cleared of snow. The school superintendent said buses would run for a regular school day. The one good thing about that was that clearing weather meant snows would probably melt on the mountainside and the boy would be less likely

to leave tracks. That would make it harder for
someone to follow him.

D.J. said his prayers, read his Bible, and dressed
without enthusiasm. In spite of everything he told
himself, he was concerned because he was thinking
of returning to the mine.

He bundled up to go outside and feed Hero. His
little dog nearly twisted himself in two with happiness
at seeing D.J.

"Hero," the boy whispered, "I'm not doing it for
me! I'm doing it for Dad and Two Mom; even for Pris.
They won't have much of a Christmas unless I find
out for sure about that mine!"

Hero licked the boy's face and whined, sensing the
troubles making the boy unhappy. D.J. absently fed the
dog and stood a moment watching him eat.

"At worst, if there is no more gold," D.J. mused
more to himself than to the dog, "I have two premium
nuggets worth more than $1,000. But that isn't
enough! Well, it won't be by the time I pay my tithe!"

He felt glum as he sat down to breakfast. His
father was more cheerful than he'd been the night
before. As everyone held hands prior to saying
grace, he made an announcement.

"Hannah and I lay awake a good part of the night,
thinking and praying. My faith was a little shaky then,
but I'm fine now. As spiritual head of this home, I
believe Brother Paul's right. God has already given us
everything we need. I'm going out and find that—
whatever it is. Now, D.J., would you ask the Lord's
blessing on this food, and to give me guidance as I
look for work today?"

The boy squirmed and protested in a barely

audible voice. "I don't feel like it, Dad."

D.J. kept his eyes on the empty plate, but he was keenly aware of his father's gaze.

After a second's silence, Dad said quietly, "Hannah, would you?"

Two Mom prayed briefly but with feeling. D.J. squirmed when she finished because he saw both Dad and his stepmother looking questioningly at him.

Dad took scrambled eggs as Two Mom passed the plate. "D.J., something going on you want to tell us about?" he asked.

The boy shook his head, but avoided his father's eyes. D.J. took a small helping of the eggs and passed them on to Pris.

Dad asked, "You and Alfred have a fight?"

D.J. noticed that his father was speaking much better English than he used to. The boy had a hunch that might be because Two Mom had been gently urging her husband to set a good example for their children.

D.J. shifted uneasily in his chair and didn't look at his father. Dad waited. Finally, D.J. answered.

"Sort of, I guess."

"What about?" Dad demanded.

"I . . . I can't tell you."

"Why not?" Dad's voice was firming up.

"Because . . . because we swore each other to secrecy."

Dad's voice came like a slap. "What kind of a secret?"

Two Mom said gently, "Now, Sam, boys have to have their secrets, you know."

"Unless it's dangerous!" Dad replied. "D.J., does

this involve something like that?"

D.J. hesitated. He didn't want to lie, but he didn't want to say too much, either. "I'm careful," he said evasively.

Dad's voice was very suspicious. "You didn't answer my question, D.J."

The boy absently stirred the eggs with his fork. "I . . . I just can't, Dad!"

Two Mom spoke quietly. "D.J., as your stepmother, I'm in a delicate position. I know you're used to having quite a bit of freedom for exploring and roaming these mountains. But the Lord has also entrusted you to my care with your father.

"Now, if you want us to continue letting you have such special freedoms, your father and I need your word that you'll not do anything foolish or dangerous."

D.J. didn't answer. He took a quick bite of Two Mom's homemade scratch biscuit* to stall for thinking time, but that didn't work.

Dad said, "My wife's right, D.J. You hiding something?"

Before the boy could answer, the telephone rang. It surprised all the Dillons. They didn't get many calls, especially so early in the morning. Two Mom was closest, so she stood and answered the call.

D.J. felt Dad's probing eyes on him, but the boy wouldn't look up.

Two Mom put her hand over the receiver. "Sam, John Milford is calling from the little store near where they live."

D.J. felt his heart jump. Had Alfred broken his promise and told his father? Was John Milford calling to pass on that information to his dad?

Two Mom added, "John says he's got an order for some firewood. He has all the equipment and wants to know if you can help him saw and split a cord this morning? He'll give you half of what the wood sells for."

Dad clapped his powerful hands together and jumped up to take the phone. "John? I'll be there soon's I get my coat and hat. And—thanks!"

Dad hung up and let out a little yip. "Thank God, we'll have some cash tonight. As for you, D.J., we'll finish this conversation later."

The word had an ominous sound. Still, the boy was glad to be off the hook for the moment.

* * * * *

The day was sunny and bright with a forecast to continue that way through the weekend. Still, D.J. didn't enjoy school even though the excitement of Christmas was everywhere. He saw Alfred from a distance, but they didn't come close all day. D.J. tried to cheer himself up thinking about the gold he'd find Saturday, for that was the day he had decided to go back to the mine.

D.J. dreaded the evening when Dad would continue their morning conversation. But Mr. Dillon came through the back door after dark whistling cheerfully. D.J. glanced up from where he was doing homework on the kitchen table.

"Guess what?" Dad called to his family, holding out a wad of bills. "A man John Milford knows had some standing dead madrone* trees that were starting to get termites. So he paid us to cut them down and sell the wood. Even after splitting with him and

John, my share's nearly $50. And when we delivered the wood to a widow woman, her neighbor ordered three cords for tomorrow!"

Two Mom ran into the circle of her husband's powerful arms. "Oh, Sam! That's *wonderful!* Why, that's better than you were making as a choke-setter."*

"After we deliver those three cords," Dad continued, separating five one-dollar bills and handing them to Two Mom, "John and I are going to drive a load over to Lake Wilderness and see if some of those rich people will buy some from us."

D.J. knew that his father meant a private community of about 2,000 people who lived behind a security gate between Stoney Ridge and Indian Springs.

Mr. Dillon continued, "Milford and I'll sit outside the gate—they won't let us in, you know—and try to sell to people driving in or out."

Two Mom opened the cupboard over the electric range, took down the sugar bowl and placed the tithe dollars in it. She said, "That sounds wonderful, dear!"

"It *is!*" Dad replied, taking off his heavy coat and hard hat. "Then I'm going to see Crabtree—remember my father told me about Crabtree sending word we could cut those trees where we used to live, D.J.? Most of the trees have been standing dead since the forest fire. Acres and acres of dry hardwood trees! Every cord will bring top dollar!"

"Why, we could easily make $800, maybe $1,000 if the weather holds clear as it's supposed to do. D.J., you can help us on Saturday."

D.J. was so surprised he slapped his hands down hard on the open textbook. "Ah, Dad!" The disappointed words exploded from the boy before he could think. Saturday was his only chance to check out the mine!

Dad looked straight at his son. "Whatever plans you had will have to be put aside, D.J. The Lord has provided a way for us to have income, and we're going to need every hand to make it pay before the bad weather comes again and we can't work!"

D.J. didn't say any more because he knew that would trigger his father's memory about the morning's conversation. He wanted to grab his homework and run to his room, but that would arouse Dad's suspicions. The boy forced himself to sit quietly, but his mind raced.

A thought suddenly exploded. He dropped his pencil and sat upright. His family was still celebrating and didn't seem to notice.

That's it! D.J. told himself. *It's the only way!*

The thought scared him. But, he told himself firmly, he was doing this for the family. He would do something he'd never done: cut school tomorrow so he could enter the mine—no matter what the dangers!

Chapter Ten

DANGER DEEP IN THE MINE

D.J. was well up Jawbone Ridge the next morning when he stopped for the seventh time to check his back trail.* His heart leaped at a distant movement below.

"Somebody's following me!"

He had carefully circled wide around the place where someone had fired the dart at Alfred and him. But the ground was soft and he'd left some tracks. It had been even worse where the bright sunshine had not yet melted the snow. Now someone was following him. But who?

D.J. lay behind a granite boulder the size of a doghouse and studied the distant figure dogging his steps. D.J. had left his black backpack on the ground. It contained 200 feet of strong, light rope, his hard hat with attached carbide lamp,* a lunch, and other items he would need in exploring the mine. He had also removed the canteen from his belt so it wouldn't clang against the bare granite boulder.

Making sure his inconspicuous gray woolen
stocking cap was snug about his ears, D.J. slowly
raised his head again and peered back down the
mountainside.

He's right on my trail! D.J. told himself. *But he's
too far away to see me. Wish I'd brought binoculars.*

He crouched and eased the backpack onto his
shoulders again. *Well,* he told himself, *he's far enough
away I can probably still give him the slip if I can
stay out of the snow and mud.*

Feeling confident of his woodsmanship, the boy
hooked his canteen to his belt and looked ahead. His
blue eyes picked out the best route. Scattered shiny
granite boulders glistened with melted snow. The sun
would soon erase any tracks he made. He just had to
be careful, jumping from one to another of the
treacherously-tilted boulders. But it was the only
way. He rose to a crouch and began running.

In half an hour, after many backward glances,
D.J. plopped onto his stomach behind a three-foot high
sugar pine log under the shadow of a black oak. He
peered cautiously through the dead branches while
catching his breath.

"No sign of him! Good!"

Hiss-thud! The deadly sound instinctively made
the boy duck. He drove his face into the brown needles
now wet with snow. A dead branch snatched off his
stocking cap.

Cautiously, D.J. looked up. A chunk of black oak
bark fell from where the metal-tipped bolt had clipped
the trunk above D.J.'s head.

*Wow! That was close! But how could he have
sneaked up on me so fast?*

Trying to control his breathing so the sound wouldn't give him away, D.J. studied the bolt stuck in the tree. From the angle it had struck, D.J. realized the bolt had come from the side and slightly ahead.

It's like being chased by a shadow! D.J. thought. *Not a sound; not a glimpse of him, and yet he not only followed me since I saw him, but he caught up with me! Where is he? I can't see a sign of him!*

The short hairs on the back of the boy's neck crawled in fright as D.J. pondered that strange event. Wild thoughts tumbled through his mind.

I shouldn't have cut school! I should have told someone where I was going! But I've got to have that gold—if it's there! The whole town needs it; not just my dad. So I've got to find out today because when it starts to snow, these mountains will be closed until April! Yet I can't let anyone follow me to the mine.

D.J.'s eyes probed for a way to move. The scene was deceptively peaceful. Except for the bolt, now silently imbedded in the tree trunk, D.J. saw only natural things. Soaring evergreens stretched up the side of the mountain toward the timberline. He'd soon be above the black oaks and chokeberries.

Overhead, the sky was clear except for two jet contrails about seven miles up. The sun was gently touching the heavily-forested side of Jawbone Ridge, making deep shadows where a pursuer could hide.

It looked so serene that it was hard for D.J. to believe that he was in such terrible danger. Yet someone was within sixty feet! D.J. pressed himself against the cold, damp earth, making himself as small a target as possible while he thought what to do.

Wish I hadn't come alone! D.J. told himself. *But*

now I'm into this mess and I've got to find a way out!

He tried to breathe quietly though his body was scalding with inner heat that urged him to run. Still, the boy knew that movement was what gave wild animals away. It was difficult to see something that held perfectly still in the wilderness.

D.J.'s eyes darted from tree to tree, from brush to shrub and from rock to downed log. Nothing!

D.J. licked his lips with a tongue that was thick and dry. He felt the cold breeze slicing across his bare head. The woolen cap swung gently on the limb where it had been snatched away.

The boy had an idea. He lay full length on the stickery pine needles and eased forward like a snake. He reached up cautiously and retrieved the cap. He clamped it between his teeth and began to crawl backward.

Slowly, expecting to hear the terrible hiss and thud, D.J. lay prone in the shelter of the log. He picked up a fallen dead limb about six feet long and eased the cap onto one end. Carefully, D.J. raised the cap beyond the shelter of the limbs.

He heard the hiss at the same instant the cap was struck violently. The bolt carried the cap out of the boy's sight.

Instantly, D.J. leaped up and began running. He crouched low, racing through the densest brush he could find, staying out of the shade of the evergreen where little growth could survive.

A crossbow's got only a single shot! D.J. told himself as he ran. *I hope it can't be reloaded as fast as a bow and arrow!*

D.J. found a shallow ravine where melting spring snows had carved a channel toward Mad River. The boy dove headfirst into the ravine and rolled down in a shower of dead leaves and sharp brown needles. At the bottom, D.J. jumped to his feet. He scrambled on up the mountainside, following the ravine's sheltering shadows.

He ran till his chest seemed about to explode and a painful stitch developed in his side. Gasping painfully for breath, he staggered on till he stumbled over an exposed root of a Douglas fir. He lay panting hard where he fell at the bottom of the shallow ravine.

When his breathing was under control, D.J. carefully raised his head. He knew better than to look over the top of the root. His scalp would be exposed before his eyes could see anything. D.J. peered through a Y where the root divided. He held his breath and listened.

The forest was quiet. He wished a blue jay would scream; they were such good alarm signals in the mountains. But the boy's frantic running would have scared away any birds or squirrels that might have been around.

All D.J. could hear was the soft, low moaning of the breeze in the long pine needles overhead.

Slowly, carefully, the boy let out a breath he had held so long it had become painful. *"Think I finally lost him. Anyway, he didn't run after me very far or I'd have heard him. Sure wish I could have brought Hero with me!"*

Two Mom would have been very suspicious if D.J. had taken his dog to school. In a way, the boy told

himself, it was better that he was alone. All D.J. had
to take care of was himself.

Satisfied that it was safe, D.J. at last eased himself
up to an almost-standing position. Still straining to
hear and being very careful, he followed the ravine
to its end. After again hiding behind a sheltering sugar
pine's trunk and listening several moments, D.J.
headed purposefully toward Black Hole Mine.

As he moved, his body tense from knowing some
unknown person was trying to stay on his trail, D.J.
tried not to think what might happen when he came
back down. The bolt shooter—whoever he was—
would probably still be waiting. But this time D.J.
would circle even farther away from the area,
especially if he was loaded with the gold he hoped to
find.

Finally, after zigzagging and circling back on his
own trail, the boy was satisfied that he'd lost the man
who'd been on his trail.

When he was within a quarter-mile of the hidden
mine entrance, D.J. climbed a small black oak and
stood on the first limb. Pressing himself against the
tree's trunk, the boy looked and listened for five
minutes.

Not a human sign showed anywhere.

Satisfied, D.J. eased down the tree and continued
on a zigzag course up to the mine. He avoided the deer
trail where he'd fallen days before. He carefully
came up on the mine so he was even with where he
knew it to be. When he was within a hundred yards,
the boy again stopped to look and listen. Feeling safe,
he still eased from tree to tree, from rocks to logs to
brush. He made little more sound than a shadow.

Finally, he was within fifty feet of the brush-covered mine entrance.

Still can't see it from here, he told himself. *Not even the headframe. That's a good sign nobody else has been here. Nothing's been disturbed since Alfred and I were here.*

Slowly, carefully, the boy eased through the brush till he could finally see the rotting timbers of the headframe. In another few moments, D.J. was at the entrance to the mine.

There he paused, catching his breath and letting his eyes skim the ground in search of nuggets. There were none.

After a final look backward and all around, D.J. shoved aside the brush that hid the mine's entrance. The boy dropped his backpack. It usually held his books, but he'd left them under his bed at home. He removed the 200 feet of bright yellow rope. It was thin and light as nylon but cheaper; the hardware store man had assured D.J. the rope had a breaking strength of half a ton. It would easily support his weight if he had to lower himself inside the mine. For now, the rope would provide a way out of the mine so he wouldn't get lost.

The idea that gold was so close made D.J. forget the danger from his unknown stalker. The boy securely tied one end of the rope to a stout exposed tree root by the mine's opening. Then he reached into his pack and removed his orange-colored hardhat with the attached carbide lamp. He ignited the wick in the polished reflector. When the blue flame hissed steadily, D.J. put on his hat. The light made weird black shadows flee from the mine's opening.

For a moment, the boy hesitated, looking into the threatening black mine entrance. D.J.'s heart thumped so loudly he thought he could hear it.

The opening seemed to wait in silent threat. Or maybe it was the thought of all he'd read about the spooky mine that made D.J. swallow hard and try to slow his breathing.

His light showed the passageway went straight back into the mountain. In mining, shafts were either vertical or inclined, either going straight down, or at an angle. D.J. played out the rope and eased forward into the mine. His hissing carbide lamp touched ancient support timbers that seemed to come alive. The beams' shadows moved silently aside as the light passed.

Some bats on the low ceiling squeaked in protest as the light disturbed their darkness.

"That's good!" the boy told himself. "Nobody's bothered them, and from the droppings, I'd say they've been roosting here for years and years!"

D.J. felt confident as the beam flipped about the dark hole. Twin narrow gauge rails, very rusted, showed that at one time small hand-pushed ore cars, called skips,* had moved in and out of the black depths.

That's where the gold is, D.J. told himself, feeling his breath coming faster. *"Crazy" Calhoun wouldn't have needed the rails and cars if he wasn't bringing out rich ore with gold in it! Sure hope he didn't find it all!*

A flush of excitement swept over the boy. He played out the thin rope as he moved deeper into the mine. As long as he held on to that yellow rope, he could find his way out of the maze of passageways and drifts* that surely lay ahead.

Each step took the boy farther from the comforting light of the mine's opening. Daylight faded and vanished completely as D.J. cautiously rounded a curve in the passageway or drift about fifty feet in.

There was a total, eerie silence except for the faint sound of water dripping somewhere ahead. The boy remembered that hard rock miners had to use pumps to keep the rainwater seepage under control. With rainfall up to 80 inches a year, plus annual spring snow melt and runoff, the amount of seepage was tremendous. When abandoned, the known mines had filled with water.

D.J. glanced nervously at what he recognized as what the miners called square sets* as he passed. If they gave way, the whole mountain could fall on him! But they had held for decades; they'd probably hold for years longer.

Still, D.J.'s courage faded as his light revealed a patch of extra blackness coming up on his left side. The boy recognized it as what miners called a stope.* It was like a large room or cavern hollowed out by drilling into the mountain. D.J.'s carbide lamp showed that the extra patch of darkness was a pit. He approached it carefully. Stepping over the rusted rails, D.J. held on to the yellow rope and leaned forward.

Some kind of a pit. Must've been caused by a cave-in. D.J. told himself. *Fifty, maybe sixty feet deep.*

The sheer walls were quite wet. Miners called this slickensides. At the bottom, shallow standing water reflected something shiny yellow!

"Gold!" he breathed the word aloud. "It looks like gold! I've got to go down and make sure."

D.J. quickly but carefully tied off his guide rope. With the remainder, he made a loop under his boots. He brought the rope back to his hands and passed a section of rope over a support timber. By slowly releasing the rope under his boots, he lowered himself in an upright position over the sheer face of the pit.

About halfway down, straining to see more of the shiny yellow at the bottom of the standing water, D.J.'s own shadow suddenly leaped ahead of him at the bottom of the pit.

"Hey!" he cried in surprise.

He automatically gripped his supporting rope firmly with his right hand while his left hand whipped up to shield his eyes from a bright light above him.

He heard a voice from behind the light. "Thanks for finding the mine for me!"

D.J. saw a knife reach into the beam. He felt vibrations as the knife began sawing through the rope on which he hung suspended!

Chapter Eleven

TERROR IN THE TUNNEL

"Hey!" D.J. yelled again. His voice echoed strangely down the tunnel,* "What're you doing?"

There was no answer, but D.J. felt the vibrations of the knife on the rope continue at a faster pace.

"Stop! Don't do that!"

Again, there was no reply. Desperately, D.J. started climbing hand-over-hand up the sturdy yellow rope. "Hey! Stop! Are you crazy, Mister?"

D.J.'s own carbide lamp wasn't as strong as the big flashlight shining down on him. The two lights made dual shadows that leaped from wet wall to shored-up ceiling to the man crouching above the pit. The knife flashed back and forth, faster and faster!

"O Lord! Please! I need help!" It was barely a moan, but it was a prayer from the deepest part of the boy's being. Still puffing and pulling himself up, hand-over-hand on the yellow rope, D.J.'s lips moved as his mind raced.

"I misled my parents! I said mean things to Alfred.
I cut school! I shouldn't have entered the mine, but
the gold. . . . " His voice trailed off and he half-
moaned, "Lord, forgive me!"

A voice seemed to come from somewhere in the
passageway. "D.J., is that your light?"

The knife stopped moving on the rope. The man's
light went out. The boy's own lamp gave him his first
clear view of the man who had leaped to his feet. He
stood, half crouching, knife in hand, peering back
toward the entrance to the mine.

D.J.'s light touched the man's face. For the first
time, the boy had a glimpse of an unshaven man,
gaunt and thin, wearing an old, shapeless sweat-
stained hat.

"Ora Octavius!"

The strange recluse D.J. had met at Grandpa
Dillon's place began running back toward the mine
entrance where the voice had called D.J.'s name.

D.J. yelled, "Look out! There's a man in here with
a knife!"

The distant voice came again, echoing before it
faded into the tunnel.

"What?"

D.J. didn't recognize the voice. It was distorted by
the narrow, echoing chambers before it vanished in the
depths of the mountain.

"I said, 'Look out!' There's someone else—"

He didn't finish before the distant voice called
again. "D.J., I know you're in here! Why'd you turn
your light off? You playing games with me?"

"Alfred?" D.J. puffed, nearing the top of the pit in
his frantic climb for safety.

"No, I'm not Alfred! Turn your light back on!"

D.J.'s carbide lamp showed the yellow rope inches above his head. The yellow strands were snapping faster and faster as his weight and furious motions completed the work begun by the knife!

"Oh, no! Please!"

He clutched the rope under his left armpit and wildly thrust his right hand above the lip of the pit. He grabbed blindly for the rails he remembered were there. His gloved forefingers touched the near rail, but D.J. couldn't get a good grip.

In a frenzy of fear, D.J. hitched himself up higher with his left hand. Dimly, he heard his name called again just as the final strand broke!

The boy groped desperately over the top of the lip, thrusting both hands out toward the rusted rails he still could not see.

The broken end of the rope hissed past his ear, sailing out over the black pit toward the far wall. Out of the corner of his eye, D.J. saw the rope sag. He heard it fall past him and plop into the water at the bottom of the pit.

The gloved fingers of both hands were clutching the rails. The lip of the pit was cutting cruelly through D.J.'s heavy coat sleeves, but he didn't care. He dug his boot toes into the sheer face of the precipice and shoved.

A second later he threw his right leg over the ledge. Pulling mightily with both hands against the rail, D.J. hoisted himself to safety. He rolled across the rails, ignoring the pain, until he struck the far wet wall of the stope, away from the pit. His heavy boot kicked against a support beam. It creaked a moment.

D.J.'s hard hat with the hissing carbide lamp had been knocked off while crossing the rails. The beam swept the tunnel ceiling, settling on an ancient crossbeam resting across the upright support D.J. had accidentally kicked.

The boy barely noticed. "Whew! Thank You, Lord!"

D.J. lay for a moment, gulping air into his tortured lungs. He felt like an empty paper sack that someone had blown up and popped.

"D.J.?" The voice was closer now. "What's going on? I can see the reflection of your light."

Suddenly, a terrible realization struck D.J.

"Look out!" he called. "There's somebody in here with a knife! He's turned off his light and is coming at you in the darkness!"

D.J. shoved himself up on one elbow. He swung his feet in a wide circle to bring them under him so he could stand. His right boot again struck the ancient upright timber.

A tiny trickle of debris slipped from behind the overhead ceiling timber where it joined the upright beam D.J. had dislodged.

For a moment, the terrible meaning of the little dirt and rock trickle escaped the boy. He was thinking only of what was about to happen in the tunnel nearer the entrance where Ora Octavius was slipping through the darkness toward someone. A second spurt of dislodged debris fell through the carbide light's beam toward the tunnel floor.

Slowly, like a slow motion film, the aged overhead crossbeam cracked and started to fall away from the support beam. But that beam, freed of the other's weight, leaned dangerously. Then, faster and faster, the rotting timbers fell toward the passageway floor!

"CAVE-IN!" D.J. yelled.

He grabbed for his hard hat with attached lamp, but the broken crossbeam whooshed past the boy's face and struck the lamp a glancing blow. The hat sailed crazily into the air. The tumbling lamp made wild shadows leap in every direction.

Then the lamp fell away from D.J., deeper into the tunnel, past where the upright beam had just crashed to the rails. The hat landed upright so the light showed against the shiny wet wall across the pit.

D.J. didn't dare try to recover the light which showed debris falling from every part of the passageway ceiling. The sickening cracking of more falling timbers and support beams made D.J. turn toward the distant drift.

He leaped to his feet, stumbled over a rail and almost pitched headlong into the pit again. His flailing left hand struck the yellow rope he'd tied off at the pit's edge. The support beam had broken and the rope was slack, but D.J. clutched wildly and held on.

"Whoooahhhh!"

He threw himself backward from the pit and kept his feet by pulling the slack out of the guide rope. D.J. regained his balance and slipped the yellow strand under his left armpit. He reached out and grabbed the rope with both gloved hands.

"Come on, feet!" he whispered. "Move! Move!"

He trotted back along the passageway, away from the terrible pit, away from the comforting carbide lamp, guided by the rope sliding through his gloved hands.

He heard voices ahead around a curve in the tunnel. Behind him, more rotting timbers creaked and groaned.

Methane gas! The thought exploded in D.J.'s mind. Mr. Kersten's words went off like a string of firecrackers in the boy's thoughts. *Rotting vegetation or timbers. Odorless. Tasteless. Deadly poison gas. Explosive!*

"Look out!" he yelled, stumbling over the now-invisible rails in the darkened tunnel. "Cave-in! Poison gas! Get out! Get out! It's liable to explode!"

D.J.'s desperate cries echoed hollowly in the black passageway. The sound seemed to be sucked up by the mine so that the words didn't go anywhere.

Only the comfort of the rope running through his gloved hands and under his armpit gave D.J. any hope. He stumbled and fell to his knees, but the rope stayed under his arm. He recovered his balance, gripped the unseen rope again and staggered on toward the invisible safety of the tunnel's entrance somewhere ahead of him.

D.J. seemed to be getting farther away from the sound of falling timbers and cascading debris behind him. But the boy didn't slow or check to make sure; he panted through the darkness toward light and safety—but it didn't seem to come any closer.

From that direction, words came through the darkness. "D.J., I can see you coming now! I can just make you out with my light! But why don't you answer me? Why don't you turn on your light?"

D.J. didn't dare stop running. He yelled through the blackness, "I'm back here! Deep in the mine! Look out—"

D.J. didn't finish the sentence. If that wasn't Alfred calling to him, who could it be?

"Of course!" The words escaped D.J.'s lips as he puffed through the blackness of the passageway guided by the rope. "Of course!"

Now it made sense! The other day, before finding the gold, he and Alfred had seen someone following them. Later, sure they'd given him the slip, the boys had been fired on with a bolt. Today, D.J. had seen someone following and again, against all logic, someone had been close enough to fire two bolts at him.

That's how! There were two people! D.J. thought, his lungs burning from the fury of his running. *One far behind both times; one closer both times!*

And they had to be Ora Octavius and Nails Abst! The man had been closer—he'd fired the bolts. He'd tried to cut D.J.'s rope. Nails had come along later, oblivious to the terrible danger he now shared with D.J.

D.J. thought he could see a faint hint of light as he rounded a curve in the tunnel, still guided by the rope.

"Nails! Look out! He's got a—"

His shout was broken off by a startled cry just ahead. "Hey! You're not D.J.!"

The surprised words passed D.J., bounced off the underground passageway walls and vanished into the blackness under the mountain behind him.

"Nails! Watch out! Run!"

"Hey!" Nails' voice came again. "What're you doing with that knife?"

D.J. heard heavy footsteps echoing along the tunnel. He knew Nails was running back toward the tunnel opening, his too-big boots clomping noisily. At the same time, D.J. saw the faint light lessen as Nails raced for safety.

D.J. stumbled on, guided by the rope, rounding a final curve in the drift.

"Thank God!" The light at the tunnel entrance burst upon D.J.'s eyes like a glorious sunrise.

Two silhouettes were moving through the passageway, one right behind the other.

D.J. was so tired and panting so hard he didn't think he could even make it to the entrance. But the domino effect of the falling and breaking timbers deep within the mine gave him one final burst of energy. He dropped the rope and charged, head low, down the last few feet of the tunnel toward the opening and daylight.

D.J. was blinded by the contrast of light from the outside and the blackness of the mine, but he could see well enough to realize what was happening.

Nails had reached the mine opening and rushed outside. There he was trapped against the dense undergrowth. Nails was facing the mine entrance, backing away, his hands held protectingly in front of him.

Ora Octavius was half crouched, breathing hard, advancing purposefully toward Nails who backed into a downed log and couldn't retreat any more.

There were voices, but D.J. didn't pay any attention. He hurled himself from the mine entrance and dove, head first, toward the back of the man's knees.

D.J.'s right shoulder hit solidly against Ora's left knee. The man went down hard. D.J. saw something bright and shiny fly from the man's hand and sail through the air. It landed in the brush beyond the downed log.

Nails had tripped and fallen. D.J. leaped to his feet, ignoring Ora Octavius, who had not moved from D.J.'s flying block.

"You OK, Nails?" D.J. asked, bending over the fallen town bully.

"I thought he was you!" Nails voice was a croak. "I was splitting wood this morning when I saw you and followed . . . but I didn't know he—"

"It's OK," D.J. said softly. "Talk later. Help me tie him up."

D.J. saw Nails' eyes open wide at the sight of something behind him.

D.J. whirled, expecting Ora Octavius to be upon him. The boy was surprised to see the man racing toward the mine entrance.

"Hey!" D.J. yelled. "It's starting to cave-in!"

"The gold!" Ora Octavius cried without looking back. He ran toward the tunnel. "I found it! After all these years, I found it! I've got to get it!"

D.J. sprinted after the man. "You can't go in there! The timbers are breaking! There'll be gas and my carbide lamp is—"

He didn't finish. There was a bright flash inside the mine. The blackness vanished and the interior of the passageway was clearly visible. A second later, there was a dull *BOOM* from deep under the mountain. Debris shot from the tunnel opening.

The concussion knocked Ora down first, then D.J. The boy tried to get up, but his ears roared and his legs wouldn't obey. He glimpsed heavy dust and debris spewing out of the mine opening and coming at jet-plane speed toward him.

But D.J. still couldn't move. Something thick and black seemed to have grabbed him. He seemed to be falling, falling down into something. He tried to stop himself, but he fell down . . . down . . . into total darkness and silence.

Chapter Twelve

OUT OF THE BLACKNESS

Slowly, D.J. began drifting up from unconsciousness.
There was a great roaring in his ears. That was mixed
with voices, but they made no sense. They babbled,
saying things without words; making only sounds that
sounded human, yet had no meaning.

Higher, very slowly, the boy drifted up from the
blackness where the concussion had knocked him. D.J.
wanted to open his eyes, but they were too heavy, too
tired.

Vaguely, he sensed something passing between
his eyelids and the sky overhead. He seemed to feel
someone bending over him. D.J. didn't know if it
was a dangerous person or not, and he couldn't think
clearly enough to react.

"D.J.?" The voice seemed to come from a very
great distance. "You all right?"

The boy didn't recognize the voice. He tried to
open his eyes to see who it was, but he was still drifting

slowly upward; still only partly conscious. What had happened? Something . . . bad. But what? It wouldn't come to mind.

D.J. heard someone at his head where it rested on the ground. He felt hands reaching under his back and curling through his armpits to rest on the front of his shoulders. Alarmed, he wanted to cry out, but he had no power for speech.

Dimly, as though it were happening to someone else, the boy was aware that he was being dragged backward by his shoulders. He felt his bootheels bang loosely against debris and brush, but there was no sensation of bumping or pain.

Only his hearing seemed to work, and that imperfectly. *Must be dreaming,* he thought wearily. *I hear my dog barking away off someplace. Must be running a trail. And that sounds like Dad. And Brother Stagg . . . and Alfred. . . .*

A grayness like dawn slowly eased through his closed eyelids. A sort of mist seemed to float before his eyes. He tried again to open them. He heard rapid footsteps as though someone was running, but D.J. was still being dragged backward by his shoulders.

He felt a final tug on his shoulders and then the dragging stopped. His shoulders were released and he rested full length against the damp earth.

"D.J.?" The voice seemed to come from a very far distance. "Wake up! Wake up!"

"Huh?" D.J.'s voice sounded strangely weak in his own ears.

"D.J.! Did you say something? Talk to me!"

The voice was closer now, almost in his ears. Slowly, with great effort, D.J. opened his eyes a crack.

He wanted to say, "Where am I?" but the words wouldn't come.

He forced his eyes open wider and then closed them instantly. But he had glimpsed the sky overhead and the soaring tops of evergreen trees against Jawbone Ridge. And somebody—a boy?

D.J.'s eyes popped open to stay. He tried to sit up, but his body seemed paralyzed. It wouldn't obey his thoughts.

"D.J., can you hear me? Can you, huh?"

"I . . . hear you. But I can't . . . move." His voice was so low and weak it sounded strange in his ears.

A shadow moved across the sky. The trees disappeared and a human face peered down on him.

"Alfred?" he asked uncertainly, trying to clear the last of the mists from his eyes.

"I told you—I'm *not* Alfred! Don't compare me with that little four-eyed character!"

The annoyance in the voice chased away the last of the fog. D.J.'s eyes focused on the face above him.

Slowly, the features took shape: an unwashed face with scars and bumps as though a herd of horses had run across it. The face was surprisingly narrow for such a stout body. D.J. got a whiff of a heavy winter coat. It smelled like a wet dog.

"Nails!" Upon recognizing the older bully who had always made life miserable for him, D.J. automatically drew back. He jerked himself to a sitting position and scooted backward in the dirt. His back hit some brush and he stopped abruptly.

"Fine thing!" Nails Abst growled, pushing himself from his knees to his feet. "I save your hide and you jerk back from me like you was snake-bit!"

D.J. blinked in surprise. His mind was clear and his vision was fully restored. He glanced around. He was in front of the Black Hole Mine, but it had changed. Where there had been a threatening entrance there was now a great pile of debris.

"You . . . you did *what*?" D.J. asked, swallowing hard and slowly getting to his feet.

"I pulled you out of that mess after the mine blew up! That's what I done! If I hadn't, you'd be buried up to your neck in that stuff! But do you care? Nah! You ain't no more thankful than that other guy was!"

D.J. looked around quickly. "Ora Octavius! He tried to cut my rope! Where is he?"

Nails pointed with his chin toward the debris spilled outside the mine entrance. "Guess you mean him. I dug his face out so he can breathe, but soon's I freed his arms, he began hitting at me with his fists. So I left him to cool off, and he passed out. Still is, I think. I'll need help to get the rocks and things off his legs."

D.J. heard a low moan. He glanced toward the sound and saw Ora Octavius.

"Sounds awake now," D.J. said.

He saw that Ora's hat was gone. His face was scratched, bloody, and dirty, but he feebly waved his hands.

"Help me!" The words were weak. "Help me, boys! I think my leg's broke!"

D.J. slowly got to his feet as his strength returned. "Come on, Nails. Let's see if we can get him free."

"He's out of his gourd, D.J. He was babbling something about gold before he passed out awhile ago."

The gold! D.J. had forgotten. He glanced toward the mine entrance—or where it had been. Now there was only a dirt slide that had buried the mine opening under tons of rock and debris.

The boy was no judge of mine disasters, but he didn't see any way the Black Hole Mine would ever be entered again. The whole mountain seemed to have fallen upon it. Somewhere under that mass of rubble some shiny objects in a pool of shallow water were also buried—forever.

But they couldn't have been nuggets, D.J. realized, because placer gold was never found in hard rock mines. Then where had D.J.'s nuggets come from?

He glanced around as he and Nails approached the moaning man with his legs buried in debris.

Suddenly, D.J. stopped and stared. His eyes darted along the ravine, then swept the side of Jawbone Ridge. It was very faint, but there were signs that water had eroded the side of the great mountain a long time ago.

"What'cha looking at, D.J.?" Nails asked.

"Huh? Oh—I was just thinking. See that funny-colored seam of earth running along the side of the mountain?"

"I don't see nothing."

"Doesn't it look as if it could have been made by a stream of water running along there? Maybe it's an ancient riverbed or a creek."

"Just looks like the side of a mountain to me," Nails grunted.

D.J. looked again and nodded. "Yeah, maybe you're right." But D.J. stole another look at the strange markings. If it had been an ancient riverbed, that would explain the nuggets he'd found. And there might be *more!* But there was no time to think about that now.

The two boys began pulling debris from the man's legs.

"Who is this guy?" Nails asked. "He came at me out of the tunnel; didn't have a light. Had a knife, I think, but it's gone now."

"Name's Ora Octavius," D.J. said, testing to see if the man's right leg could be lifted from the mess. "I met him at my Grandpa's."

"What's he doing here?"

"Chasing a crazy dream, I guess."

"Yeah? What kind?" Nails tossed the last piece of rock away and reached to take the man's hand.

"He had gold fever," D.J. answered. "Thought he'd discovered a gold mine he'd been looking for over many years."

"Well, he sure won't find it around here, D.J. No gold around here a'tall! Here, let's get him on his feet."

D.J. bent to help Ora Octavius stand. He made it, but immediately doubled over and almost fell.

"OH! My leg!"

Nails kneeled to check it out.

Ora's bleary eyes focused on D.J. and recognition came.

"Didn't mean to harm you none!" he said.

Nails stood up. "Probably busted his leg. Let's get him to that log where he can sit."

"No harm a'tall!" Ora repeated to D.J.

"You could have fooled me!" D.J. said as he and Nails helped Ora hobble toward the log. "In fact, you could have fooled me good when I was hanging over that pit in there and you were cutting my rope!"

"Just wanted to scare you—that's all." The man's voice was low, almost pleading.

D.J. and Nails lowered the man to a sitting position on the fallen log.

"You did that all right!" D.J. admitted. "Scared me when you shot those bolts too!"

"Didn't hit you, though, did I? Could've if I'd a'wanted."

Nails asked, "What's he talking about, D.J.?"

D.J. ignored Nails to answer Ora. "You hit my stocking cap dead center!"

"Proves my point!" the man exclaimed, touching his fingertips to his bloody face and looking at the fingers. "Don't you think I know the difference between a cap with a head in it and one stuck up on a stick?"

D.J. had bent to check the man's leg, but glanced up to meet Ora's eyes.

"Guess you'd know the difference, all right. But the rope was cut nearly through so it broke!"

"Wouldn't have if this here other kid hadn't surprised me, yelling like he did in the drift! Made me jerk the knife and cut deeper'n I intended. I swear I was just going to stop and threaten you; make you promise never to come around again!"

Nails obviously didn't understand what was going on. He said, "My pop's got one of them bolt things. Lets me shoot it now and again."

Ora Octavius didn't seem to hear. He looked at D.J. and said, "That's *my* gold, you know! Been looking for it for years! Read all about 'Crazy' Calhoun's mine, and figured it had to be somewheres nearby. Soon's my leg's well, I'm a'going to reopen that there mine and dig out the ore! Be richer'n anything! And you know what, boys? Since you helped me just now, I'll let you watch me do it!"

D.J. smiled and then started to laugh.

Nails asked, "What's so funny?"

"I recognized somebody else in what he just said!"

"Yeah, who?"

"Me," D.J. said. "Well, not anymore. Hey—listen!"

Hero's sharp, loud bark echoed off the mountains and voices blended with it.

"It's my dog!" D.J. cried, looking back toward Stoney Ridge. "And my dad and Brother Paul and Alfred! There they are! Topping that rise! We're going to need them because of his leg!"

D.J. waved and yelled. Hero let out a glad explosive bark and raced toward D.J. Dad, Brother Paul, and Alfred hurried down the hill toward them.

Then it hit D.J. How did they know he was here? There was only one logical explanation—Alfred had told! But had he given away the secret about the gold or just the place where D.J. might be? Right now, it didn't matter—D.J. was glad to be alive.

D.J. turned to Nails. "I want to thank you for saving my life. Twice, in fact. Once in the drift and out here when you pulled me away from the entrance. If you hadn't, that slide could have buried me alive."

He didn't say anything about having just again saved Nails by making a flying tackle against Ora when he had Nails backed up helplessly against the dense undergrowth. Apparently, Nails didn't think of that either.

Nails rubbed a dirty hand over his chin. "Good thing I followed you when I seen you ditching school this morning. Didn't see this guy, though. Not until we were in the mine, then he jumped me and I ran out here just before the explosion."

"Thanks," D.J. said quietly.

"Guess that makes us even, D.J. You saved my bacon back when that outlaw bear was about to get me."

D.J. slowly nodded, remembering. "Guess it does," he said. He turned to face the people rushing down the hill. "And I guess Alfred told about our secret, or he'd never have led Dad and Brother Paul here."

"What secret? What're you talking about, D.J.?" Nails asked.

"Nothing. Just thinking. Guess Dad was right— there's a time when it's dangerous to keep secrets."

D.J. looked at what was left of Black Hole Mine. Whatever mystery it had held all these years was still safe. "Crazy" Calhoun's secret was buried under the mountain along with any gold that might have been there.

D.J. started walking uncertainly toward the oncoming party. Hero outran them and leaped up on D.J. with joyous barking as the boy bent in front of him. D.J. gently ruffled the mutt's scarred ears.

Dad called, "You all right, D.J.?"

"Everything's fine, except this man's got a broken leg, I think."

Brother Stagg's big voice rumbled up from his deep throat. "I'll look after him, Sam. You see to your boy."

Father and son looked at each other for a long time. D.J. saw Dad's jaw muscles twitching.

"D.J., I've got a good mind to give you the thrashing of your life! You did a terrible thing!"

"I know, Dad." D.J.'s voice was barely a whisper.

"Grounding you isn't enough—you know that! But you're grounded except for Christmas shopping with Two Mom or me! You're not going anywhere alone until the New Year! Meantime, I'll think on what other punishment is proper for doing such a thing! You hear me?"

D.J. lowered his head and barely nodded. "Yes, I deserve every bit of that," he whispered.

Dad was silent for a moment, then added more gently, "Don't you EVER scare us like that again!"

"I won't, Dad. I promise."

Dad took such a sudden step forward that D.J. automatically jerked back. In Dad's pre-Christian days, he would have whacked D.J. backhanded and "clean into next week," as Grandpa had once said.

Instead, D.J. found himself engulfed in his father's arms. For the first time in a long time, D.J. was crushed in a powerful, caring hug.

D.J. glanced over the top of his father's wide shoulders and met Alfred's eyes.

Dad let him go and stepped back, blowing his nose noisily in his big blue pocket handkerchief. D.J. walked up to Alfred. He had been standing some distance away.

"Alfred, I did a bunch of dumb things, and I'm sorry. Forgive me?"

Alfred replied sheepishly. "D.J. . . . I told your dad and Brother Paul because I thought you'd done a crazy thing and might be in danger. My father would've come to help too, but he was—"

D.J. interrupted impatiently. "It's OK. Can you forgive me?"

Alfred grinned. "Sure! Friends again?"

"Friends," D.J. said, reaching over to playfully punch Alfred on the shoulder. "Oh—here."

D.J. dug into his pants pocket and pulled out both nuggets.

"Here! You take the big one!"

"Wh . . . at?"

"It's yours! I'm going to cash in this other one and give Nails half of the money. With the rest, I'm going to buy the best Christmas presents my family ever had!"

Brother Stagg's mighty voice broke through D.J.'s excitement. "Reckon I've fixed up this leg about as good as I can under the circumstances."

Dad nodded. "Then let's get out of here while there's some daylight! And while we're going, D.J., you can tell us what happened today."

The boy did that, but that night he had to repeat it for Two Mom and Pris. Later, he had to tell Grandpa. By then, everyone wanted to hear, so Two Mom set a night one week before Christmas when everyone who wanted to could come to their home.

A CHRISTMAS TO REMEMBER

The little house was packed with people from the church and all over Stoney Ridge. But D.J. looked mostly at the familiar faces: Dad, Two Mom, Pris, Grandpa, Alfred, his parents, and the Staggs. Elmer Kersten, the newspaper editor, had driven up from Indian Springs and brought his press camera.

Nails Abst was there too. His father had been invited, but he didn't come. D.J. was surprised that Nails had accepted. It was the first time D.J. had ever seen Nails with a washed face, combed hair, and a clean shirt. D.J. guessed that Nails wanted to be there when the story of what happened at the mine was retold, since Nails was the hero.

"Well," D.J. said when everyone urged him, "one more time!"

D.J. told the whole story from start to finish, including finding the gold nuggets, the way the gold changed his attitude, right down to the cave-in and

115

Nails rescuing Ora Octavius and D.J.

When the boy had finished, everyone clapped and whistled and shouted. Except Two Mom. Her eyes were misty and her hands flew nervously about.

To cover her deep feelings, she reached toward the coffee table and picked up an old shoe box. She opened the lid and gently lifted out a decorative star. It would fit at the top of the ceiling-high Christmas tree the family had picked out that afternoon.

Two Mom's voice broke. "The Lord has done more than we asked or dreamed," she said softly. "Having Mr. Crabtree give so many of us all that firewood to cut and people to buy it. Enough money for us to have a joyous Christmas and work on into spring. Sam, would you step up on the ladder and place this star so we'll be reminded of the Star of Bethlehem?"

Wordlessly, Dad took the ornament and climbed three steps of the aluminum ladder. He settled the star into place.

Pris snapped on the switch and the whole tree burst into light.

There were a few soft gasps of appreciation, then Two Mom continued. "Maybe by springtime the tourists will start coming to walk in to see the Black Hole Mine. People will come from all over to see such a sight, you know."

Kathy Stagg shook her red-gold hair in the habit she had. "I heard a couple hundred thousand people a year go through some of the places like the Empire Mine in Nevada County! As long as they walk, they won't hurt the environment here! Everybody wins! Isn't that right, D.J.?"

He looked at her and smiled. "Everybody except
Mr. Octavius. From what Mr. Kersten tells me, he'll
have to stand trial even though he claims he didn't
intend to hurt Alfred or me."

"Or me," Nails said.

The newspaper editor snapped two pictures in
rapid succession before agreeing. "Gold fever can
sneak up on a man, they say. I guess Ora just got too
much and went slightly whacky. But no harm done, as
it turns out—except to the mine."

Alfred pushed his thick glasses up on his nose and
looked around at everyone. "Guess the only one who
lost is old 'Crazy' Calhoun. But maybe he didn't
either. Nobody's ever found his gold—probably never
will—if it ever existed."

D.J. reached into his pocket and felt only lint at the
seam. He'd sold the gold nugget and divided the money
with Nails as he'd told Alfred he would.

"Maybe there's more where Alfred and I found
that," D.J. said, thinking again that maybe an ancient
stream bed had once coursed down Jawbone Ridge.
When the snows melted in the spring, he and Alfred
would check it out—but not in secret. D.J. added,
"After all, maybe what they say around here is true:
'Gold is where you find it.' "

"But even if there's not another gold nugget on
Jawbone Ridge," Grandpa said with a shake of his
Irish shillelagh, "we'uns turned out to have the best
Christmas in a 'coon's age!"*

D.J. listened to the laughter and then glanced out
the picture window. Snow had been falling for some
time. Every bush and tree was softly molded into
beautiful white shapes. It looked like a postcard

Christmas.

Alfred eased up to stand beside his friend. "You ever see anything so pretty, D.J.?"

"No," D.J. answered softly. His mind leaped over the small community of Stoney Ridge to Jawbone Ridge. Some questions flickered across his mind.

Alfred seemed to read D.J.'s thoughts. "What'll happen to the Black Hole Mine now? I mean is it going to stay buried forever under all that debris, or should it be dug out and reopened?"

D.J.'s heart speeded up at the thought of the mine being uncovered again. Maybe "Crazy" Calhoun's original quartz gold vein would be found! Or more placer gold would be discovered in the ancient riverbed like the two nuggets D.J. had picked up.

"You know, Alfred, maybe we should file a claim on the old streambed—just to be safe. And the mine area too."

Alfred glanced around, then whispered, "I thought you'd given up on filing any claim."

"I'm not thinking about the gold. I was thinking more of what Two Mom and Kathy said about tourism. Can you imagine what would happen to our town if that mine area could be made into a tourist attraction?"

Alfred's eyes glowed thoughtfully behind his thick glasses as he began to catch the vision. "Kathy was right about a couple hundred thousand people touring the Empire Mine grounds each year. Of course, that's a state park, and they've got old buildings and things there that the Black Hole Mine doesn't have."

"But," D.J. interrupted, "if Stoney Ridge only got a fraction of 200,000 visitors a year, think of what that would do to this whole area!"

D.J.'s excitement was growing. "Visitors would buy souvenirs, visit stores and shops in town, eat meals; all sorts of things! We could start a museum! Maybe the lumbermen who lost their jobs could make a living right here, without having to move. . . ."

He let his thoughts trail off.

"What's the matter?" Alfred asked anxiously.

"We'd need money to excavate the site. Who would pay to put in a hiking trail to the mine? How would the workers get paid?"

"Maybe they'd volunteer," Alfred said hopefully. "They'd get a lot back if it worked."

"That just might work, Alfred! So maybe we'd better file on the claim right away to protect our rights. Then we'd have until the snows melt off Jawbone Ridge next spring to think about how to do all those things."

"We?" Alfred asked softly.

"Sure! We're friends and share everything, don't we?"

Slowly Alfred nodded. "Yeah! Then, you and I would get the money raised from tourists' admissions to the mine!"

D.J. grinned. "Now who's getting gold fever?"

Alfred returned the grin. "OK! OK! Anyway, you could write a history of the Black Hole Mine. I'd help you with the research. Mr. Kersten could print it as a booklet at the newspaper office. Then we'd sell it like a souvenir."

"Alfred, that's a *great* idea!"

"That part would be our own money, maybe enough for college someday."

D.J. snapped his fingers and grabbed his friend's skinny shoulders. "You know what?"

"What?"

"We could set up a historical nonprofit organization so everyone in Stoney Ridge would benefit. I read about something like that one time in Mr. Kersten's newspaper. Or we could even try to get the Black Hole Mine made into a state park!"

For a second, Alfred hesitated, then answered. "That'd be best for everyone, wouldn't it?"

D.J. nodded, feeling very good inside. Silently, he turned to look out the window again and thought about when his mother had been alive. But she was gone, and this was D.J.'s first Christmas with a new family. Everything changed, it seemed, and yet Christmas didn't.

"I wonder what it was like that night in Bethlehem," D.J. said quietly.

Two Mom spoke softly, "Sam, do you think everyone would like to join hands and sing Christmas carols?"

"I was just thinking the same thing, Hannah. Come on, folks. Gather round!"

D.J. entered the circle, holding Alfred's left hand and Kathy Stagg's right. D.J. smiled at them, thinking.

Brother Paul's deep bass voice started and the others joined in. "O little town of Bethlehem. . . . "

D.J. sang from a full heart, realizing he had almost missed ever having Christmas because of what he'd done in trying to solve the mystery of the Black Hole Mine.

But that was past, and this was going to be a Christmas to remember! D.J. was *sure* of it!

* * * * *

Across town, unknown to D.J., his favorite schoolteacher was reading a letter that had arrived with the afternoon Christmas cards. Soon D.J. and Alfred would again be in great danger because of their next exciting adventure with the **Ghost of the Moaning Mansion.**

LIFE IN STONEY RIDGE

NAILS ABST: D.J. met Nails in *The Hair-Pulling Bear Dog*.

ADRENALIN: A term used to describe the feeling of a warm rush through the body when someone is frightened or upset.

ARMY SURPLUS: Retail stores that sprang up after World War II to sell excess military equipment, clothing, and supplies. Such stores have changed somewhat since then, but basically they still offer the same kind of merchandise to customers.

AVOIRDUPOIS (pronounced "Av-Urd-Uh-**Poiz**"): A series of weight units based on the 16-ounce pound.

BACK TRAIL: A term from the Old West meaning to examine where the person has been to make sure no one is following.

BATCHING: Slang expression for a man who lives alone as a bachelor.

CARBIDE LAMP: The type of light usually found on a coal-miner's hard hat. The light comes from mixing water and gray-colored carbide pellets in a closed container, which makes a gas. This gas is released through a small hole into the reflecting chamber, which is mounted on the hard hat. A spark from a flintwheel ignites the gas and creates the light.

CHOKE-SETTER: A lumberman who prepares downed trees for the heavy equipment that will take the trees out of the woods. The choke-setter digs a hole or tunnel under the downed tree trunk. Then he throws a strong steel cable over the log and pulls it back through the hole. He puts the knob on one end of the cable through a loop on the other end and pulls the cable tight around the log. A tread-type tractor then hooks onto the log and pulls it out of the woods.

CONIFERS: Another name for the many cone-bearing trees or shrubs. Spruce, fir, and pine trees are all conifers.

'COON'S AGE: Slang expression meaning a very long time, since raccoons were once believed to have long lives.

CORD: A measure of firewood totalling 128 cubic feet. One cord equals a stack of wood 4 feet high,

8 feet long, and 4 feet wide.

CORNISH MINERS: Most of the hard rock mining in California's Mother Lode was done by Cornish miners who migrated from Wales. They were said to be the world's best at this difficult and dangerous trade.

CROSSBOW: A 15th-century weapon made of a bow, fixed transversely on a stock. The bow string is released by a trigger. Modern adaptations and improvements have made the weapon popular in some types of game hunting.

DOCENT: Originally a college or university lecturer, the term is used in the California state park system to mean an unpaid volunteer. This man or woman may lead a tour, explaining a particular subject, such as mining, to visitors.

DOUGLAS FIR: A large forest tree growing up to 300 feet tall, erroneously called Oregon Pine. Douglas fir is considered the most important lumber tree. It has cones 2 to 4 inches long. Young trees are typically pyramidal at the crown with horizontal and sometimes drooping, lacy branches. A pretty tree, the mature branches tend to become rounded or somewhat flattened. Small Douglas firs are commonly used as Christmas trees.

DREDGES: A small placer mining system commonly seen today in California's Mother Lode rivers. A pump forces river water over a unit on the surface.

Sluices or slanted areas channel water, sand, gravel, etc., while the lighter gravel is carried off back into the river. The heavy gold is trapped in the carpet. The carpet is removed and the gold reclaimed in a separate process.

DRIFTS: A horizontal passage underground which follows the gold vein. These are distinguished from tunnels.

FENCE: A person who receives and sells stolen items.

HAIR-PULLING BEAR DOG: A small, quick dog of mixed breed. A hair-puller's natural tendency is to go for the heels or backside of any animal, including sheep, cows, or bears. This mutt is also called a "heeler" or "cut-across" dog.

HEADFRAME OR HEADGEAR: A sort of derrick, this was a steel or timber frame at the top of a mine shaft. The headframe had a rope or cable and a pulley for raising and lowering things in and out of the mine, especially on a shaft (which was a vertical or an inclined excavation).

IRISH SHILLELAGH (pronounced "Shuh-**LAY**-Lee"): A cudgel or short, thick stick often used for a walking cane. A shillelagh is usually made of blackthorn saplings or oak and is named after the Irish village of Shillelagh.

ITINERANT: A person who travels from place to

place, such as a circuit preacher, judge, or salesman.

JUMP A CLAIM: A miner's expression for someone who tries to seize a gold mine found and claimed by another person. Early-day claim jumping was often violent.

LOST DUTCHMAN, GUNSIGHT, BREYFOGLE: Three very famous lost mines in the Old West dating back to the time of early pioneers. None of these mines has ever been found, but rumors persist that they exist, and some hopeful prospectors still try to find them.

MADRONE: A beautiful evergreen tree that grows to a height of about 80 feet. The pinkish-orange hardwood makes excellent firewood, though it usually doesn't split as evenly as oak does.

MINE SHAFT: A vertical or inclined excavation or opening from the surface.

MOTHER LODE: A term applied to the gold-bearing area in the foothill section of California's Sierra Nevada Mountains running from about Mariposa on the south (near Yosemite) to Downieville in the north. The famous Gold Rush of 1849 covered this area. Many people still find gold today in the Mother Lode.

ORE CARS: See **SKIPS.**

OUTLAW BEAR: This reference is to an event

told in the first D.J. Dillon Adventure, *The Hair-Pulling Bear Dog.*

PARAPHRASED LIVING BIBLE: A popular re-statement of the Bible by Tyndale House Publishers, this paraphrase gives the meaning in another form. By rewording, the meaning is intended to be made clearer.

PLACER MINING: A shallow or surface accumulation of minerals in the wash of streams, as sand, gravel, and other deposits. In California's Mother Lode country, placer mining today involves seeking to reclaim gold dust, flakes, and nuggets near or from rivers, creeks, and other streams or old water courses.

PONDEROSA: A large North American tree used for lumber. Ponderosa pine trees usually grow in the mountain regions of the West and can reach heights of 200 feet. The ponderosa pine is the state tree of Montana.

ROACH BACK: This term refers to a hump or high curve in an animal's back.

SCRATCH BISCUIT: A kind of bread made in small, soft, round cakes. They rise in baking through use of soda or baking soda. A "scratch" biscuit is made entirely by the cook without use of a prepared store-bought mix.

SKIPS: In mining days, there were two types of skips. An open iron car on four wheels was one kind. It ran on rails and was especially needed in inclines in the gold mines. Gold-bearing ore and debris (called "muck") was taken to the surface on such skips. The larger skips were pulled by mules. There were also smaller one-man skips which a recluse like "Crazy" Calhoun could work by himself.

SNOW DAY: Any school day when the county superintendent of schools may cancel classes because heavy snowfall has made running buses or conducting classes unsafe. A snow day must be made up by extending the school year another day in the spring.

SQUARE SETS: A set of timbers composed of cap, girt (heavy beams supporting the end of rafters), and post. These three timbers met to form a solid 90 degree angle. This system helped make a safe work environment which one man, working alone with no one to help him in an emergency, would have preferred.

STETSON: A broad-brimmed, high-crowned felt hat like a cowboy's. The Stetson is named for John B. Stetson, an American hatmaker who lived during the time of the Old West.

STOPE: In mining, an underground excavation from which the ore has been removed. This was like an underground room compared to the long, narrow drifts or passageways.

STRINGER: A journalism term for a part-time newspaper reporter who covers his own local area for a paper published somewhere else.

SUGAR PINE: Largest of the pine trees. Sugar pines can grow as tall as 240 feet. They have cones that range from 10 to 26 inches long and are often used for decorations.

TUNNEL: A horizontal passage with both ends open to the surface. However, as a mining term, the word is sometimes used to mean one opening at daylight and extending across surrounding rock to the vein or mine.

TURNOUTS: In narrow mountain roads where it is difficult to pass another car safely, sometimes short sections of the shoulder are paved and marked with a white line. Slower moving vehicles are encouraged to pull onto the turnouts. They keep moving at a reduced speed while faster traffic passes in the regular driving lane.

WET SUIT: An insulated, rubberized coverall type of garment that covers the whole body except for the face and hands. Divers wear wet suits to keep in body heat and stay warmer in chilly waters.

D.J. DILLON
· ADVENTURE SERIES ·

The Hair-Pulling Bear Dog
D.J.'s ugly mutt gets a chance to prove his courage.

The Bear Cub Disaster
When his pet bear causes trouble in Stoney Ridge, D.J. realizes he can't keep the cub forever.

Dooger, The Grasshopper Hound
D.J. and his buddy Alfred rely on an untrained hound to save Alfred's little brother from a forest fire.

The Ghost Dog of Stoney Ridge
D.J. and Alfred find out what's polluting the mountain lakes — and end up solving the ghost dog mystery.

Mad Dog of Lobo Mountain
D.J. struggles to save his dog's life and learns a hard lesson about responsibility.

The Legend of the White Raccoon
Is the white raccoon real or only a phantom? As D.J. tries to find out, he stumbles upon a dangerous secret.

The Mystery of the Black Hole Mine
D.J. battles "gold" fever, and learns an eye-opening lesson about his own selfishness and greed.

Ghost of the Moaning Mansion

Will D.J. and Alfred get scared away from the moaning mansion before they find the "real" ghost?

The Secret of Mad River

D.J.'s dog is an innocent victim—and so is the hermit of Mad River. Can D.J. prove the hermit's innocence before it's too late?

Escape Down the Raging Rapids

D.J.'s life depends on reaching a doctor soon, but forest fires and the dangerous raging rapids of Mad River stand in his way.

Look for these exciting stories
at your local Christian bookstore.